MAY 21

CITY ON THE EDGE

CITY ON THE EDGE

DAVID SWINSON

MULHOLLAND BOOKS

LITTLE, BROWN AND COMPANY

NEW YORK BOSTON LONDON

Copyright © 2021 by David Swinson

Hachette Book Group supports the right to free expression and the value of copyright. The purpose of copyright is to encourage writers and artists to produce the creative works that enrich our culture.

The scanning, uploading, and distribution of this book without permission is a theft of the author's intellectual property. If you would like permission to use material from the book (other than for review purposes), please contact permissions@hbgusa.com. Thank you for your support of the author's rights.

Mulholland Books / Little, Brown and Company
Hachette Book Group
1290 Avenue of the Americas, New York, NY 10104
mulhollandbooks.com

First Edition: May 2021

Mulholland Books is an imprint of Little, Brown and Company, a division of Hachette Book Group, Inc. The Mulholland Books name and logo are trademarks of Hachette Book Group, Inc.

The publisher is not responsible for websites (or their content) that are not owned by the publisher.

The Hachette Speakers Bureau provides a wide range of authors for speaking events. To find out more, go to hachettespeakersbureau.com or call (866) 376-6591.

ISBN 978-0-316-52854-2
Library of Congress Control Number: 2021935757

Printing 1, 2021

LSC-C

Printed in the United States of America

For my father, Tom Swinson

Life is a gamble. You can get hurt, but people die in plane crashes, lose their arms and legs in car accidents; people die every day. Same with fighters: some die, some get hurt, some go on. You just don't let yourself believe it will happen to you.

—Muhammad Ali

CITY ON THE EDGE

It was painstaking work, creating that fort out of a large thicket at the bottom of the hill. The opening was small and cut through the side so it couldn't be spotted by anyone who might wander by. A tall cinder-block wall, about ten feet in height, stood a few feet in front and stretched across part of the bottom of the hill and down the road toward the Corniche. It surrounded an old abandoned peppermint-stick lighthouse. The wall made for good cover and didn't restrict our view to the other side of the hill and down the same road to our apartment building, which was a couple of blocks up from the Corniche, and the Mediterranean Sea.

The fort became our hideaway. We named it Chameleon Fort because a three-horned chameleon made its home in a tree that had twisted limbs bending over the top of the thicket. In retrospect, it should have had a name having to do with scorpions, spiders, or vipers. We used large sticks to swish and bang the ground on the inside to clear out as many of the creatures as we could. A lot more dangerous than expected to build that fort, but at the end, well worth the trouble. We were blinded to all the danger. Don't know if it was stupidity or just youthful naivete.

Roddy and I spent most of our time at Chameleon Fort during the curfew. What else was there to do? No school. We were restricted, and not allowed to leave the building. But there we were. Our dads were never around, and I could only speak for my mother, not Roddy's. She was always at the apartment of a friend or in her closed bedroom, drinking and smoking cigs. Micheline—our housekeeper, cook, nanny, sometimes friend—was easy. Snuck right by her. Never a problem, and even if she did catch me I knew she would have backed me up. So Roddy and I would meet on the ground floor in the garage area, then stealthily make our way to the fort.

We had binoculars and peered out the side entrance to focus down the road toward our apartment building and the Druze village to the right of it. Sometimes we imagined we were at war with the Druze, and had to gather intel based on our surveillance; when the old woman came out to dump the bucket of dirty water in the gutter; when the young man tended to the goats, or when the little girls were playing chase on the pavement in the front area of our building. Our true enemy was Toufique, always shadowboxing in the late afternoon when the sun was high. He wasn't with the Druze, though. His grandfather, Abu Fouad, managed our building and owned the small convenience store on the ground floor by the road.

There were about fifty Druze of all ages living in homes made of tin and stone and found wood. We knew their routines well. We knew our apartment building well. All ten floors. I lived on the eighth floor and Roddy on the fourth.

We set our sights on those who lived in our building sometimes. On occasion we'd get lucky and spot a woman coming
out in a bikini or even topless to bathe in the sun. We'd
chuckle, but back then our twelve-year-old bodies did not
respond the way twelve-year-old boys would nowadays. It
was a different time, and we were just silly boys caught up
in a grand adventure. We knew right from wrong, but told
ourselves this was okay because it was war. A kind of war.
Our private war.

One late afternoon I was at the fort alone, spying. I had to
be back for dinner soon, and on that day I was supposed to
be at Roddy's apartment, so I had to get back before the call
to dinner. Couldn't take a chance Micheline (or worse, my
mother) would call the Stankeys.

Just as I was gathering my stuff and about to leave I heard
rustling coming from the area of the road near the cinder-
block wall. I peeked through the opening but couldn't make
them out. They were too close to the part of the wall that led
down the road.

Sounded like two men talking.

They stopped at the bottom of the hill, to my left and only
a couple of feet from the fort. They became a little clearer as
I peeked through a narrow separation of the vines, but only
from their chests down. One of the men had his back toward
me, the other facing him. The man with his back toward me
was dressed in dirty white baggy pants and a long-sleeved
white shirt. The other wore clean khakis. I couldn't see anything else. The man in the khakis had an aggressive tone.
He spoke in the broken Arabic of an American or Brit. His
hands were of a light complexion, not like the man with
his back toward me. The back of the other man's right hand

was darker. His Arabic was fluent, like he was born to the language.

The man with his back toward me repeated *la, la,* several times, which I understood to mean *no.* He sounded defensive.

Out of nowhere, the man who was facing me leaned into the other with force. I noticed his right hand strike the man in the chest. Sounded like a hard punch. The sound the other man made was one I'll never forget. Like something more than getting the wind knocked out of you after a sucker punch. More like something confined for years finally escaping.

He lost his feet from under him and fell, his face inches from my position. He had a thick black beard and square-rimmed glasses. I recognized him.

His glassy eyes open wide. *Does he see me?*

He gurgled several words and released a breath like a long sigh. Blood from the corner of his mouth bubbled out and quietly burst to something like a teardrop that streamed down to get caught up in his beard.

PART ONE

ONE

The murder of the Middle Eastern man was the first homi-cide I ever witnessed. I still consider him my first body, because you never forget the first one. There would be plenty more to come in my future, but nothing like that time in 1972 and '73, in Beirut, Lebanon—and watching it happen.

It was fall of 1971 when Dad requested the post in Beirut. We were settled in Arlington, Virginia, having spent four years in Mexico City. I was certain, even at that young age, that his decision to go back overseas was so that he could distance our family from the city where my sister, Dani, had died over six months ago. Unlike my totally transparent mother, the signs of something like grief or depression in Dad were never made obvious. Yes, it was difficult to see my mother go through that. I believed the move was more for her benefit. Tommy was three years younger than me. He felt great sadness but got over it. I did too, but not as fast as him.

My mother kept herself in her bedroom, drinking vodka, smoking cigarettes, and watching the portable television. Sometimes all day and night. At that point, totally incapable of looking after me and Tommy. Dad took leave before he had to go. He was a Foreign Service Officer with the State Department. Taking leave seemed to settle things, enough so that he felt comfortable with the decision.

Mother, Tommy, my bull mastiff Buster, and I were moved to a hotel in DC when Dad left for Beirut in the spring of 1972. All the furniture and our belongings were packed by movers and shipped. Everything I owned, aside from what I had in my suitcase, which wasn't much. He even took the necklace I'd been wearing for over a year from me. It had the Star of David attached to it. Mother gave it to me because of her Jewish heritage. She said that it was important that I know her family's heritage, and that the necklace would be a positive reminder.

I had a hard time with having to take it off. It's one of the only things Mother gave me that meant something. Family history or some shit like that.

"I'll keep it safe until we return to the States," Dad said.

"Why, though?"

"Why what?"

"Why can't I wear it?"

"Because we're going to be guests in another country. It's a country where the people won't appreciate this symbol on your necklace, worn around your neck."

"I'll keep it tucked in my shirt."

"No, it'll be safer this way."

"That doesn't make sense."

"It doesn't have to make sense. We have to respect that."

"Mom said it's important because it's a part of our heritage."

"That's fine. You can wear it when we get back."

"Mom told me I'm Jewish because she is."

"You're not Jewish. You're Presbyterian, like me."

"It's a blood thing, she said."

"You're a damn Presbyterian, Graham. Now hand over the necklace."

"Geez."

I unlatched it from around my neck and handed it over to him, but not without throwing him a look like I'd struck out on the third pitch.

He cupped it in his hand and walked away without another word.

TWO

The plane began its descent over the Mediterranean Sea, the water below a vivid blue-green, like glass. Even from our altitude and looking through the scuffed window, I could see the white sand and reefs at the bottom. Reefs that looked like dark stationary serpents. That's what I thought they were at first.

And then there was the land. The soil red, like clay.

Red Play-Doh.

"It's the color of the earth in this part of the world," Mother told Tommy.

"It looks like blood," I said.

"Why do you always have to be so morbid?" she said and wrapped her arm around Tommy.

"*Blood,*" Tommy said, like it was a funny word.

My mother was nursing a vodka on ice. I had lost count, but she was drunk.

I reclined in the seat, looked out the window. I thought about Buster in cargo, surrounded by luggage like a piece of luggage himself. Over eight hours. That was a long time. The longest he'd ever been crated and on a plane. The vet gave him something to help him sleep, and Dad told me dogs don't have the same sense of time that we do. He survived the trip to Mexico City and back. He'd survive this.

When we arrived at the airport, we were met by an embassy driver. He had hair cut high and tight, like he might be military, but he wore khaki slacks and a cream-colored short-sleeved shirt. He drove a black American-made sedan with diplomatic plates.

I held Buster tight on a short leash. His legs were a bit unsteady because of the sedatives. People walking by looked at him suspiciously, like he posed a danger. Some sort of monster. He was a brindle and had a big head and broad, muscular shoulders—a dog they probably hadn't seen before. Or possibly they didn't think he was a dog.

"That's a tough-looking boy," said the driver.

"He's a bull mastiff," I said.

"I thought they were taller."

"That would be the English mastiff," I said.

"Nice-looking dog. The locals will steer clear of him for sure," the driver advised.

My mother said nothing and walked toward the rear door. The driver opened the door for her. She scooted to the other side. Tommy followed. The driver went back for our luggage. It fit easily in the large trunk.

I had Buster hop in first. His back feet slipped off the seat but he was able to plop to a sitting position next to Tommy. I stepped in and sat close to Buster. I placed my left arm around Buster's thick neck, scratched the top of his broad shoulder. He was drooling. It was a thick, slow-to-drip drool.

"Yuck," Tommy said.

I wiped it away with the bottom of my white T-shirt, leaving a clear, gooey, snotlike stain.

"Oh, don't do that, Graham. That's disgusting," Mother said.

"I take care of my boy," I told her.

"Well that's noble of you, but still gross."

I rolled down the window as the driver pulled away from the curb.

The air was hot and dry, but not oppressive. Lot of different smells, unlike DC or even Mexico City. Salty sea odor mixed with spices, decay, vegetation. All at once.

We hit the Corniche, a long seaside highway that ran along a seawall with a view of the Mediterranean Sea on one side and Beirut and Mount Lebanon to the east on the other. A city on the edge of the sea. There was a sidewalk with rails on top of the seawall overlooking the Mediterranean. Pedestrians walking. Pushcart street vendors, some of them selling colorful-looking fruit I'd never seen before. Below, along the reefs, old fishermen using long bamboo poles with lines out were standing on almost every one of the craggy reefs along the bottom of the wall, the waves gently slapping the reefs and over their feet.

The sea is what held me. All these years later and I'm still there. The most beautiful water I'd ever seen. It looked like the color of what I later discovered on the beaches of Tyre to be Phoenician glass. Aqua, green, blue, and see-through. There was so much to take in along the way that it made the trip seem shorter than it probably was.

The Riviera—a tall, extravagant hotel that towered over the Corniche—was on the northwest corner of a narrow road. Every room had balconies and a view of the Mediterranean. I was excited for a moment, thinking this was where we would be staying. The driver made a right on a narrow road. The side of the hotel took up a good portion of the road as he continued up, passing the hotel. Hell, not staying there.

As he drove, the first thing I noticed in the distance, midway up a large hill, was the figure of a man wearing an off-white gown and a white tagiyah hat. He was holding a long bamboo pole up to the sky. The pole had a white rag tied to the tip. He moved the pole in wide circles, with some thirty or so pigeons flying a few feet above and following its direction. The man in the gown stood to the side of a makeshift shack.

The driver turned left onto a dirt road and parked at the edge of an overhanging garage with several parked cars underneath. A walkway led to a small elevator. A small man wearing a white short-sleeved button-down shirt, neatly pressed black slacks, and shiny combat-style boots sat on a folding chair. The apartment building was ten stories. On the other side of the dirt road, about one hundred yards below the large hill, was a small playground. It had a swing set with four swings, a long slide, and a Tetherball on a metal post. No kids were playing, but it was early evening. Sun beginning to set.

To the right of the apartment building, where the dirt road ended, was a village. Small housing made of whatever could be found extending on each side of a wide dirt walking path with a trenched-out gutter in the middle that looked like it held sludgy water. An old woman was pulling dried clothing off a line in front of one of the shacks. An older boy farther down was kicking a soccer ball up with his feet and knees and keeping it from hitting the ground. Damn good job he was doing.

The driver opened the door for my mother. I opened my side and stepped out. Buster's feet were still unsteady as he jumped out and almost took a slide on the dirt.

"You should take him for a walk. He probably has to relieve himself," Mother said. "We'll wait here."

"Okay." I scoped the vicinity for a good spot for him.

There were large cement steps that led up the hill to some other large apartment buildings and what looked like a road. The man with the pigeons was on the right side of the steps and far enough away that I didn't worry about bothering him. The paved road we had turned off became a dirt road that ended at the hill. On the other side of it was a cinder-block wall; a few yards between it and the dirt road had shrubs and tall grass. I walked him there.

I turned to notice a local boy who looked to be in his early teens—older than me. He was at the front of what appeared to be a small convenience store attached to the building, with a large window display that had Arabic writing on the wall above it. The boy watched me intently. Out of nowhere, he began throwing air punches in my direction, trying to show off some fancy footwork, like he was Muhammad Ali. I was and still am a fan of Ali, so I know his shuffle, smooth and quick. The boy was neither. It was odd and I should have seen it, but I was just a naïve boy. That kid, Toufique, would soon become my mortal enemy.

Buster took a long piss, squatting like a girl dog. Urine traveled down the edge of the road so strong it cut through the dirt.

THREE

The man sitting on the chair was the concierge. He held the elevator door open for us. The driver helped with our baggage to the eighth floor. We stepped out of the elevator to a hallway. There was one door on the left and another on the right. Only two apartments on the floor. He led us to the right, set the luggage down, and reached into his front pants pocket to retrieve a set of keys. He unlocked the door, handed my mother the keys, and carried the luggage into the foyer.

"Your husband asked that you give him a call when you arrive," the driver said. He reached into his shirt pocket and pulled out a card. "This is where you can reach him. Would you like me to take your baggage to the rooms?"

"No, thank you. You've done more than enough."

"This is a beautiful city," he said. "Paris of the Middle East. Enjoy."

My mother smiled, found the dial phone on a corner table in the foyer, and called our dad.

I unlatched Buster from the leash. He looked around, sniffed and moved toward the living room, smelling the ground as he walked.

It was a large apartment. The living room had a huge sliding-glass door that opened to the balcony. The dining room was on the left, and to the left of that was an open door to what looked like a small bedroom. There was a single bed in it. *Dang, I hope those aren't the rooms we'll have.* All our furniture was there. I walked into the living room while my mom was talking to Dad. There was a large den on the left with another sliding-glass door. My dad's bar was in there, along with shelves of books and his stereo and reel-to-reel system.

I was anxious to know where my room was. Tommy joined me in the living room. There was a hallway to the left of the foyer, and I assumed that was where the bedrooms were.

"Let's check out the hallway," I said.

He followed.

To the right was a bedroom at the corner, with an eight-by-ten piece of paper taped to the door and MASTER BEDROOM written on it. To the left was another room that had Tommy's name, and to the left of that a door with my name on it. At the end of the hall on the left of my door was the bathroom. Another *dang* because I might have to share the bathroom with Tommy.

I could hear my mother in the foyer.

"I'm very tired," she said. "I might be in bed when you get home. Yes, I'll make sure they're settled in. We ate on the plane so I'm sure they are fine."

I hit the left toward my room.

"Buster," I called out, and he followed.

I opened the door to my bedroom, told Tommy to go away to his own bedroom. "The door that has your name on it."

He frowned, not wanting to go in there alone.

"I can wait," he said.

"Go on now," I ordered, and he walked away back to the foyer.

"Can I take Buster?"

"Negative," I told him. "He's with me 'cause this is his room too."

I'm sure the hallway seemed at the time much longer to Tommy than it really was. He dragged his feet across the carpet, pouting.

"Baby," I mumbled.

I didn't know it then, but I was jealous. After Dani's death, Tommy got all my mother's attention. It was like I wasn't there unless I was getting in trouble.

I opened the door. My bedroom was in several boxes—six medium-sized, and one larger wardrobe box. It's not like I had years of personal property collected. I was happy my dad had left everything for me to put in place. There was my double bed in the center of the room, facing my dresser drawers with a mirror in the middle. A small empty bookshelf was to the left of it. Across the room were open curtains, and a sliding-glass door that opened to the wraparound balcony. I could see the hill above the playground, with the steps carved up along the center. The man with the pigeons was gone.

I opened the sliding-glass door and stepped out. Buster followed. To the left was a privacy wall that separated this balcony from the neighboring one.

"All these new smells for you, boy," I said, looking down at him. He was sniffing away, poking his nose as much as he could between the rails of the balcony's fence.

I walked to the right, where the balcony wrapped around our apartment to the dining room. On that side was a view of the striped lighthouse surrounded by the cinder-block wall, and the Mediterranean Sea. The sun was setting, casting a beautiful blue-orange sky over the horizon.

"That's the Mediterranean Sea," I told Buster. "Give that a smell. It's something." I breathed it in.

A man's voice cried out the Islamic call to prayer over a megaphone at a nearby mosque in that moment. It was hypnotic—calming and peaceful. I was excited to be there.

FOUR

On the day my older sister died, my mother was in New York City visiting relatives. She took Tommy with her because he was young, and my dad had to work. Dani and I, mostly Dani, were at the age where we could take care of ourselves until Dad returned home from work, not so much Tommy. It was summer vacation. And I say mostly Dani, because she did look after me. I was not responsible. I was not a good boy. I'd go through a whole box of Cap'n Crunch in a sitting, an hour before dinner. I also had a way of finding trouble, or rather finding myself getting into trouble. Dani had a way of convincing me otherwise when she realized what it was I was about to do. Hell, I don't remember how after all this time, but she did. Nowadays? What the fuck does that mean? A box of Cap'n Crunch. I'd like to think I had a certain rebellious nature, always questioning my parents, most of the time to the point of punishment.

On the Sunday my mother was to return, my dad wanted to take a drive to Great Falls for a hike.

We never made it.

Dad always took the long way because he liked to drive.

We drove along the George Washington Memorial Parkway toward McLean. The Potomac River ran east of the parkway, down a sloped wooded area. There were no homes on the side of the river between Key Bridge and the CIA headquarters, a structure not visible from the parkway anyway.

Dad always drove fast—not so much in the city, but when the parkway was open like I-66 or I-95 he took advantage of it. I was in the back seat, behind Dani in the front, and was focused on the river, thinking how cool it'd be to get a boat out there one day. "Nice-sized bass," my father had told me a while back. "One day we'll rent a boat and get to it."

Only a few other cars on the parkway. He took a bend in the road, and all I remember—a terrible, vivid memory—was a large buck jumping out high from the trees. The front end of the car clipped him hard. Dani screamed. I did too. I noticed my dad's right hand instinctively stretching out to hold Dani. When the car skidded, he brought his hand back to the wheel. Like the gunfight I was in when I was a rookie uniformed officer, everything was slow motion at first, then like a quick fast-forward to the end. The buck was taken over the hood of the car, its antlers then head and long neck broke through the front window on the passenger side. That's when Dad lost control of the car and it took a dead spin down the slope into the woods. Stopped hard by a large tree before the river.

I didn't know where I was when my eyes struggled to open. Everything was blurry, but the bright fluorescent lights still burned through my lids and partly opened eyes. I could make out two figures standing at the foot of the bed. It sounded like they were speaking from an old radio, which made no sense. The one with a white coat broke away from the other and stopped at the side of the bed. He shined a little flashlight in one eye, then the other, repeating it several times. He said something to me, but I went out again.

Georgetown Hospital was where we were taken. My dad spent several nights in my room. He had stitches on his fore-head above his left brow and a Band-Aid on the bridge of his nose and his right hand was covered in tiny dried-up cuts. I think I saw my mother two or three times and I figured she was with Dani while Dad stayed with me.

It wasn't until I finished high school, years after everything I'm telling you, that I learned how she died—impaled by the buck's antlers.

What were the odds of that?

Shit.

Time catalyzed the pain and disaffection my parents felt for one another, set them on their destructive course, and how my mother felt about and loved me (or didn't), because I'm the one who survived. It was like a grenade thrown into the core of the family.

FIVE

Dad returned home early from the embassy. He had Lebanese take out. We ate at the dinner table. Nothing like having a shawarma for the first time. Not the same thing in the States. I've found places in DC that come close, but still not all there.

"Who's going to live in that little bitty room near the kitchen?" Tommy asked. "It has its own bathroom."

"It's a great room for you," I tried to encourage him so I wouldn't have to share a bathroom.

"No, no," said my dad. "That will be for someone like Raquel in Mexico. Someone to look after you guys, the house and cook."

"I miss Raquel," Tommy said.

"Yeah, me too," I said.

"Yes, I think we all do," my mother said.

Dad smiled. Hadn't seen him smile for a while.

Buster scooched his way under the table between our feet, settled near me—the sucker who'd always pass him something on the sly. And I did: a nice chunk of lamb from the shawarma. He was a bit too loud eating it.

"Don't feed the dog," Dad said. "He has his own diet. There's a service through the embassy where you can set up interviews," he advised my mother. "Do you want me to take care of it?"

"I'm capable," she told him in an ill-natured way. It was the kind of tone that could set anyone off, even my dad, who always was a patient man unless rules were broken.

"These are really good," I said, knowing where the conversation was likely to go.

"I got them from a little place on a popular street named Hamra. The stone steps at the hill behind the playground lead to it, but I drove." He took a bite and after swallowing said, "We'll all go soon, take in the sights. You'll get to know the area, like you did in Mexico City. It's gorgeous here. The Paris of the Middle East."

After dinner I was excused to go in my room and start unpacking. Buster stayed at the table. I rinsed off my plate in the large kitchen. There was a door with large glass windowpanes to the left of the counter and the sink. I looked through. It opened to a smaller balcony with a view of the rear of the building and a vacant lot strewn with large rocks, cinder blocks, and portions of walls, including a large archway with a torn white curtain still attached. The remnants of a demolished building. The lot was surrounded by a cinder-block wall that appeared to be about five feet in height.

All the boxes had my dad's nearly perfect handwriting on the top identifying the contents—books and comic books; games and assorted toys, records, and stereo equipment; clothing and so forth. I took a chance with games and assorted toys because I was hoping to find my binoculars.

I got lucky.

I pulled them out. Had this urge to spy. It was dark, but several apartments in the buildings at the top of the hill had their interior lights on. I peered through the binoculars, following the darkness of the hill upward until I spotted a lit building.

"What are you doing?" my dad asked from behind.

I jumped. Didn't expect him there.

"Checking out the new neighborhood."

I know now that he more than likely thought otherwise. But I was just spying. I loved to spy. I didn't have those certain urges that were soon to come. Girls undressing. Shit like that. My intentions were far from that. I was more interested in mentally noting what people were doing and turning it into some sort of adventure. It was a new country, after all.

"It's dark. There's nothing to *check out*. You can do that when it's daylight, so put the binoculars on the dresser and get busy unpacking."

"Can I set up my stereo and listen to music?"

"Yes, but only with your headphones."

"Cool."

"Cool, sir," he countered with a smile.

"Cool, sir dad."

He snickered and walked out. He never expected me to say *sir*, despite his military background before the State Department.

I opened the box that contained my stereo equipment. It was an all-in-one. The turntable was connected and on top of the receiver. A see-through plastic hood covered the turntable. All I had to do was plug it in and hook up the two desktop speaker wires to the back of the receiver. I chose my five-drawer dresser to the left of the attached mirror as the spot because the large headphones had a long wire that could reach to the floor at the foot of my bed. That is where I loved to sit, stretch my legs out, and listen.

I found my small collection of records. About twenty 33s and a dozen 45s. Everything from The Archies and Jethro Tull to Three Dog Night and Velvet Underground.

Buster found his way into my bedroom, plopped down to rest his big head on my leg. I got lost listening to Three Dog Night. Every song was always a different story in my head. It helped pass the time, especially if there was no television. In Mexico City all we got was *Tarzan* on a portable black-and-white television. The time difference was starting to hit me. Almost fell asleep listening to "Never Been to Spain." It was early, but I couldn't wait for the next morning. Ready to explore outside. I got myself set for bed.

The curtains were left open. The bright sunlight broke through my eyelids. Buster worked his big body onto my double bed, his forelegs stretched over my chest. I nudged him hard.

"Get up, boy."

He lifted his head, yawned.

I hopped out of bed, all the energy in the world and ready to put it to good use.

SIX

We have several boxes of cereal in the pantry," my mother said when I walked into the kitchen. She was sitting at the round kitchen table sipping coffee beside Tommy, who was already chowing down on a bowl.

"Dad here?"

"He left early for work."

I opened the pantry, saw several cans of dog food on the first shelf. It was Alpo, just like we had in the States. I grabbed a can.

"There a can opener?"

"I believe in the top drawer to the left of the sink."

There were two dog bowls on the floor at the other end of the counter, near the door to the balcony. One was full of water. Dad always thought ahead. I opened the can for the anxiously awaiting boy and spooned it out into the bowl. He ate like he hadn't had food in ages. Gone in seconds.

I found myself a box of cereal and a bowl. Poured it high. Four scoops of sugar and half a bowl of milk.

"This milk tastes weird," I said after the first bite.

"Something we'll have to get used to again, I suppose," she said.

"I got a lot of stuff unpacked last night," I lied. "Can I go out and explore after I get dressed? Check out our neighborhood?"

"Me too," Tommy jumped in.

"It's hardly our neighborhood. No. Not until your father shows you around. We don't know what's safe."

"Dad already said it was safe."

"You can take Buster for a walk, but only to where you went the other day. No farther. No exploring. Understood? When he's done his business, come straight back."

"Geez."

"Can I go with him?" Tommy asked.

"No!" Then she realized it was a bit too harsh for her dearest and said, "No, sweetie. I need you here with me."

He frowned.

"And I mean it, Graham."

"I know."

It was just another place for me. I knew it was far from our homeland, but I had no worries. It was different for my mother, I suppose.

After getting dressed, I put Buster's leash on.

I stepped out of the elevator to the parking area that opened to the road. Most of the cars were gone. Some chickens were running around the village area, and an older woman wearing a clean white headscarf covering her face was out collecting eggs. The village was clean even though it was run-down. Blankets for curtains in the windows, tarps or shower curtains to keep a roof from leaking.

I was thinking I got up too early for most of the kids, and that's hoping there were other American kids in the building.

Made me nervous. The little convenience store was closed too, but the man with the pigeons was on the hill exercising them. That hill was calling my name. And the sea across the Corniche begged for me. I took to the water, having swum in the Gulf of Mexico, Veracruz, and Acapulco. I was all about snorkeling. Dad taught me at an early age.

After I took it all in and the boy did his business I returned to the apartment so Mother wouldn't get pissed off, thinking I was disobeying and roaming around.

After lunch I returned to the bedroom, looked at the boxes left to be opened. I wanted to get things organized but wanted to go out more. It was boring.

The doorbell rang.

I about jumped out of my socks because I hadn't heard a doorbell for a while. Buster let out deep threatening barks right away, already claiming the apartment as his own. He ran to the door ahead of me. I got there just as my mother was looking through the peephole.

"Would you take him by the collar, please?" she ordered.

I did. His barks turned to protective growls.

She opened the door.

"Hello, Sanderson family," said a lady and another man in unison.

With them were a boy who looked to be about my age and a little girl. The boy had a plate of cookies piled high and covered with some sort of plastic food wrap. The lady had a bottle of something with a large cork. The man was holding two champagne glasses in each hand.

"Well hello," Mother returned politely. "I'm Sandra."

"I'm Beth Stankey, and this is my husband, John, son William and my daughter Sarah. Just thought we'd welcome you to Beirut. I hope we're not disturbing you." She looked down at Buster. "He's a large one. Friendly, I hope."

"Not bothering us at all. And yes, he's friendly. He thinks he's a lap dog. Please, come in."

"I brought sparkling wine. It's not too early for you, is it?"

"I didn't know if your husband would be home so I brought four glasses," John said.

"I'm sorry. He's at the embassy."

"Well, more for us, then," he said with a goofy smile.

"Yes, it's never too early for good sparkling wine."

The parents stepped in, followed by the kids. My mother closed the door, double-locked it.

"This is Graham," she said patting my head like she would Buster, "and behind me is Tommy, my youngest. My husband, Carl, is with the embassy here. Oh, but I said that already."

"John here is a high-school English teacher at ACS."

I looked the son, William, over. He was skinny, had dirty blond hair cut over his ears and was wearing a white T-shirt and cut-off jean shorts. His dad also had longer, dirty blond hair. He wore bell-bottom pants and a loose-fitting untucked white T-shirt.

"Hey," I said to the boy.

"Hey," he returned with a nod.

"Let me take that from you," my mother said to William.

He offered her the plate of cookies.

They were invited to the living room, where Mother placed the plate of cookies on the coffee table and took the wrapping off. Tommy immediately ripped into the pile, taking more than his little hand could hold. At least four. Mother said nothing.

"We can open that in the kitchen," my mother said.

Mrs. Stankey gave her the bottle and followed her to the kitchen.

"Why don't you children go play?" Mother said.

I grabbed three cookies.

"Just two," Mother said.

"You can grab more," William's dad whispered.

We did.

"I got stuff in my room," Tommy advised Sarah. She looked like she was a year or two younger, but that didn't matter at that age. She picked up two cookies. They both ran to the bedroom. We older boys were a bit cooler than that.

Their son kneeled down to pet Buster on the head.

"What's his name?" he asked.

"Buster. Buster Owen Sanderson."

"Quite a name there," said the father.

"We have a dog too. Nothing like this beast, though."

We heard a *pop* from the sparkling wine. The mothers returned shortly after.

"I go by Bill, by the way, not William. Friends here call me Roddy, though."

"Why Roddy?"

"My middle name is Roderick. It just stuck, you know?"

"Cool. Wanna go to my room?"

"Sure." He nodded.

We walked. Didn't have to run like little kids.

SEVEN

You bring anything special from the States?" Roddy asked.

"Just what's in the boxes. I guess my records and comics."

"No, I mean American candy, like Hershey's, M&Ms, stuff like that. You telling me you don't have anything?"

"No. 'Fraid I didn't. You can't get that here?"

"Not a thing. Not even Bazooka. Best they have here is sugar candies and candied fruits and weird ice cream."

"You gotta be kidding me."

"No. No." Like it was the end of the world. "That's a pact we all make here—you go to the States for vacation, you go with a list. We all pay good for it, too."

"Okay." I said then, "Wait a sec." I dug in my left front pant pocket, pulled out an old squashed Tootsie Roll. "You can have this. Been in my pocket for a while, though."

"You kiddin' me?"

"No. It's yours."

"How much you want?"

"Nothin'. We'll call it square 'cause your mom brought these cookies."

I handed it to him.

"Darn. Thanks. He couldn't unwrap it fast enough. Even left a bit of paper stuck to it. He smelled it, then gently dropped it in his mouth, savored it between his cheeks before biting.

"Dang, man, I don't think I can swallow this 'cause then it'll be gone."

I chuckled. As he chewed it slowly, his face couldn't help showing how much he enjoyed it.

Friends for life now.

Still licking his chops, Roddy went to my dresser, started looking through the records.

"You ever listen to America?" he asked.

"No. Heard of them, though."

"I got a record of theirs. I'll let you borrow it. They're cool."

"All right. I got this box here. It's full of my comics and books."

He knelt down, looked through the two piles of comics with a "Yep, yep, okay," and an "Oh yeah" when he got to The Hulk but then a deft "Huh?" when he reached The Archies.

"Naw, those are old. I keep them, though, because I don't like throwing my stuff away."

"Yeah, I can see that."

"What floor you on?" Changing the subject.

"Fourth. Not as good a view as you."

He stood, walked to the sliding-glass door. I opened it and we stepped out. The man with the pigeons was not there.

"They call those Stinky Steps," he said, pointing to the large stone steps that led up the hill.

"That's a weird name."

"Not really. They really do stink. A lot of the spots are

up those steps. The Arab men walk up, get drunk silly, and when they return, they piss, vomit, even take dumps along those steps."

"Gross, man."

"Yeah, I don't recommend going up those steps or on the side of the hill where the Pigeon Man is."

"I've seen him. Pretty cool how he gets those pigeons to follow the ribbon."

"That might be cool, but he isn't. We all made the mistake of going up that hill and being chased back down by him, sometimes even with a machete."

"Seriously?"

"Yeah, I'm serious. Two Lebanese kids went missing about a year ago. Word is their parts are buried somewhere above that shed he keeps for his pigeons."

"Parts?"

"Yeah, parts. Most of them got chopped up and fed to the pigeons."

"Now you're just playin'."

He looked at me direct. "I'm not. That's the word and I for one am not going to take a chance and think otherwise."

"Dang."

We went back to the room.

"You like Three Dog Night?"

"Yeah."

"I got one of their records on the turntable if you wanna hear."

"Sure."

I put the needle on. It skidded a bit and played, but I remembered I had the headphones plugged in so I unplugged them and quickly turned the volume down.

I sat on the foot of the bed.

"So what's the school like here?"

"School is school, but not so bad. There's more freedom at ACS. It's like being in a boarding school without boarding there. They do have boarders, though. Mostly older kids. How old are you?"

"Twelve."

"Me too. So seventh grade, right?"

"Yep."

"It's not so bad."

"And what about the beach down there?"

"Hah! That's far from a beach. It's all reefs. There's the pool that belongs to the hotel, though. That's cool. The closest thing they have to a beach here is rocky instead of sand. You have to wear flip-flops if it gets hot or you'll burn the skin off the bottom of your feet."

"Some places sand will do that too. So you can't swim in the ocean?"

"*Sea,*" he corrected me.

"I know. I'm just used to saying *ocean.*"

"I never said you couldn't swim in it. There's spots away from the fishermen that are pretty primo."

"You snorkel?"

"Heck yeah. I wouldn't go in those waters without knowing what's down there. I also have a nice speargun."

"Cool. Never done that."

"I'll teach you if you want."

"Heck yeah." A moment of pause, then, "What's with the Lebanese boy in front of the store down there—thinks he's Muhammad Ali or somethin'?"

"He thinks he's Muhammad Ali," he laughs. "But all he can

do is sting like a butterfly and float like a bee, so that's why most of us call him Butterfly Boy."

We both laugh.

"But he's another one you have to watch out for. He'll throw rocks at you from behind a wall. I got hit in the head once. Hard. I'm not talking pebbles, either. He hates Americans."

"Why?"

"Don't really know. Heard my dad talking to a guy he works with once when they were on the balcony. My dad said something about some Muslims hate Americans because of what we stand for."

"That doesn't make sense."

"Yeah, but I'm pretty sure Toufique is one of those Muslims, so watch out."

"Dang, seems like there's a lot we have to be on the lookout for around here."

"Oh yeah. For sure. But all the fun you'll have'll more than make up for it."

EIGHT

Roddy and I became good friends in nothing flat. Partly, I believe, because it was toward the end of summer vacation and most American families were still Stateside on vacation. There was no one else to hang out with. Regardless of that, we still would have been tight because we thought alike, especially when it came to music, comics, and especially war and police games. And, of course, spying.

"Boobs at one o'clock," Roddy blurted.

I fixed my binos to the left of Roddy, on the opening to Chameleon Fort. Found his one o'clock. Quickly took them from my eyes.

"That's my mom, you blockhead!"

He laughed a high-pitched laugh, not like a girl, but like a boy whose voice was beginning to change. Crackled.

"Ha! Mommy boobs."

I twisted his nipple.

"Ahh," he cried.

"That'll teach ya."

"Dang, man. That hurt."

"And you hurt my damn eyes."

"You said *damn*."

"Damn right."

I felt like I'd done something bad, seeing my mother's bare breasts for the first time. I tried to shake the image from my head, but it kept coming back. The image of it still does, after all these damn years. I thought about sticking my finger down my throat to puke or something, just to show the blockhead how sick that was, and to hopefully make me feel better.

"Crap, that's not even funny. And keep it down or you'll draw attention to our location and blow our cover."

He peered through his binos again and said, "Dang, I can't believe your mom sunbathes topless."

"Shut up." I knocked his binos with my hand, so they almost fell out.

He chuckled.

"Check out the playground," I said.

He focused on the playground. Toufique was shadowboxing to the side of the swing set where Sarah and another little girl were swinging low, kicking their toes at the ground to keep the momentum.

"Keep an eye on him," said Roddy. "That's my sister."

"Yeah, roger that."

"You think you could take him?"

Tell the truth, I hadn't really thought about it. I had never been a fighter. I learned how to fight almost fifteen years later in the police academy. Learned even more when I was on the street.

"Heck yeah. Kick his butterfly wings to the dirt." I cupped my mouth with my hands and sang quietly, "Float like a bee, and sting like a butterfly. Float like a bee, and sting like a butterfly," then we laughed. "I could kick his ass, but then my dad'd kick mine."

That would always be my excuse not to fight, pretending to be afraid of my father's wrath before anything else. Not really an excuse, though. My dad was a firm believer in self-defense, not starting the fight. That's against his rules.

We watched as Sarah and the other little girl left the playground, headed toward the building. Toufique was gone too, but we hadn't noticed him leave. *Fine stakeout this was.*

"I feel like getting a shawarma. Let's go to Hamra, then."

"Sounds good," I said. "But I have to ask my mom."

"Guess I should too. You wanna hit it, then?"

"Yeah."

Saying *Let's go to Hamra* was the equivalent of saying *Let's go to Sunset Boulevard.* It was always crowded, and stuff was always happening. Best shawarmas in the city were on Hamra Street.

We packed up the binos in a little knapsack, along with a couple of thermoses that contained orange soda. I peeked out the opening to scan the area.

"Looks clear," I said.

We slowly made our way out, heading toward the wall and the dirt road, crouched all the way.

I always wanted to be a cop. I read detective-story comics and war stories, and got a hold of some of my dad's paperbacks, like Wambaugh, MacDonald, and Graham Greene, who I always thought I was named after because he was Dad's favorite author. He didn't really write crime fiction, but the spy stuff was worthy of my attention. I learned a lot from those books. Developed some good games, too. I'd mostly play them out in my head, though.

We were on the road above the playground and walking toward the apartment building. Out of nowhere little rocks were being flung at us. I got hit on the right lower back. Damn, it stung.

"Yeow!" I blurted.

We turned toward the direction of the rocks that were being hurled. It was to the left of Stinky Steps behind a big thicket, a good fifty yards. They were zipping fast, like more than one person. We had to dodge most of them. Damn good aim.

"Run!" Roddy cried out.

We hauled ass toward the building. I was struck again, but this time on the back of my leg. I noticed the rock bouncing down the road ahead of me. They were about one inch in diameter, not enough to kill you, but more than enough to cause pain and injury.

Yes, I wanted to be a cop. One thing I knew for sure about cops was they never ran from danger, they ran to it, seeking cover along the way. They weren't stupid about it, though. That's what I wanted to do, even entertained it for a second or two—grabbing larger rocks along the way until I found good cover and then chucking them in the direction of the threat. Maybe get a good head-shot. Then another one pelted me on the back side of my bony left shoulder, and that was enough to get me running faster. Had to be using a slingshot, but the rocks were coming too fast. Would have to have one darn strong arm. Or maybe there were two of them.

Didn't ever realize how fast Roddy was. He was already at the garage area, waving me on like I was about to make a goal.

"Hurry up!" he yelled at me.

I nearly tripped on the edge where the dirt road turned

to pavement, regained my balance and made it to Roddy. We chose taking the stairs because it was faster. Before entering and having achieved good cover, we looked back one last time to see if anyone was running out of the large thicket.

No one. We both had a strong feeling about who it was, though, and there would be revenge.

Guaranteed.

"*Kol khara!*" Roddy yelled to the guy we knew was out there.

An old lady in front of her shack at the village scowled at us.

"What does that mean? What you yelled?"

"I don't know—but it's bad, I know that. Got in a lot of trouble for saying it at home once."

"*Co harra!*" I screamed, but not quite the same pronunciation.

At the stairwell before we hit the stairs, I stopped Roddy and said, "This stays between us. No parents. No grown-ups at all. Understood? If it's a battle, you don't tattle."

"Man, this is pretty darn serious. He could've knocked one of our eyes out."

"Then we'd come up with something. If it's a battle, you don't tattle. That's all I know."

"Yeah. Okay."

We ran up the stairs.

NINE

When I opened the door to the apartment, Buster was there to greet me. He was always there to greet me, slobber and all. I called out for Mother. Tommy ran out of his room.

"Mommy's not home."

"Where is she?"

"Your mother is out visiting with Mrs. Stankey," Micheline told me in a thick accent.

Micheline was the one my mom decided to hire. She was from the Seychelles Islands. Had no family. She did not smoke or drink. She was very religious. Believed that Jesus Christ was her Lord and Savior. Remembering what my dad said, I didn't tell her my mother was Jewish, so that made me Jewish, and that Jesus was just a great man and a prophet, nothing more. The Messiah had not arrived. It's not that I necessarily believed that then, it was what I was told.

Micheline always wore a sleeveless dress cut just above her knees with colorful island-type flower patterns, and blue flip-flops. Pretty sure she didn't wear a bra. Her skin was dark and shiny to perfection. Not one blemish that I could remember.

There did come a time that I did look. Yeah, I looked. Her hair was kept like an afro but tied with rubber bands at the ends so the ends were like little twists. I liked her. We all did. Especially my mother. They would often sit in the kitchen and talk while my mother drank coffee and smoked cigarettes. Well, mostly my mother would do the talking and Micheline would be the attentive listener. Despite liking her and respecting her as a new family member, I did not feel like I had to ask her permission, so I just told her, "I'm going to Al Hamra with Bill to get a shawarma."

"Me too. Me too," Tommy jumped in.

"No, you can't go," I said. "Mom won't allow you."

"Just ask her."

"No. It's just gonna be me and Bill."

"I like you here with me, sweetie," Micheline said to him. Then, to me: "And I think you call and ask your mother."

"I'm sticking around here for a few until Bill shows up. He's asking his mom, so if Mom is there, she'll know."

"No fair," Tommy said.

"Nothin's fair, knucklehead."

"You come in the kitchen with me. I will cut up some delicious fruit."

Tommy shot me a frown and then followed her into the kitchen.

"You tell me when you go," Micheline said while walking.

"Come on, boy," I told Buster and walked into the living room to wait for Tommy.

I looked out the sliding-glass door to the sea and thought how I'd have to hit the reefs soon, before school started. About five long-pole fishermen stood on the reefs. Traffic along the Corniche was busy as usual, with a few pedestrians walking along the sidewalk and looking over the rail along the seawall. The land was growing on me. I loved it more than any other place we had lived, including Mexico City in the sixties, which was hard to beat. Like here, there was so much freedom for a little kid. Nothing like nowadays.

The doorbell rang a few minutes later. Buster was the first one there, barking and jumping.

Tommy ran out of the kitchen, followed by Micheline. I got to the door after Buster, peered through the peephole.

Roddy.

I held Buster by the collar and opened the door.

"What's up?" he said.

I shot him an upward nod, closed the door and let go of the beast. Buster bolted toward Roddy, almost knocking him down. Roddy grabbed him around his thick neck and wrestled him until Buster knocked him to the floor and slobbered him.

"Oh yuck, man. Stop, beast."

"You're his new buddy," I told him, but really meant play toy.

He managed to shove Buster away and get up.

"Down, boy," I commanded.

He sort of obeyed.

"Hello, Ms. Micheline," Roddy said respectfully and with a large smile.

"Hello, boy," she said returning a smile.

"Hi, Bill," Tommy said with too much enthusiasm.

"What's up?"

"You boys stay on the sidewalks when you get uptown," Micheline said.

"We will," I promised

She escorted Tommy back to the kitchen. He was reluctant

but obeyed. Bothered me at the time, how much he wanted to hang with us. As far as I was concerned back then, he was nothing but a pain in the ass and a mama's boy. In fact, I was surprised he wasn't at the Stankeys' with my mother.

"What'd your mom say?" I asked.

"No prob."

"My mother say anything?"

"Not a word."

"Figures, but I'll take it as a yes. Want to go in my room first? I wanna scope out the area where Butterfly was throwing the rocks."

"Yeah, makes sense. Need to make sure it's safe."

Trying to be as clandestine as possible, we ducked down and opened the sliding-glass door and crawled out to the balcony, gripping the binoculars. We got on our knees when we reached the guardrail and peered over.

"It was over there, just over the playground to the left of Stinky Steps," Roddy said.

"I know."

I rested the binoculars on the top rail, checked out the area. There was a good view over the thicket where the rocks were coming from.

"I don't see anyone."

"You sure?"

"Yeah, I'm sure."

"You think our fort is blown?"

"I don't think so. He didn't start throwing the rocks until we were close to the playground." I directed the binoculars to where Chameleon Fort was. "Not a good vantage point to our fort from where he was."

"You sure?"

"Yeah man, I told you I'm sure. You want to go?"

"Let's see those binoculars."

"What, you don't believe me?"

"I do, but I just want to see for myself."

"You gotta trust your partner."

"I trust you, G."

He handed me the binoculars and said, "Let's go."

We crawled back in. I closed the sliding door, crawled a bit more, and stood. On the way out, I grabbed a few lira from inside my top dresser drawer.

"Ha. Now I know your hiding spot."

"And now I know who knows." I smiled.

I patted Buster on the head.

"Be back soon, boy," I told him. "Be back in a while," I called out to Micheline.

TEN

Walking up Stinky Steps took my breath away. Literally. I was only twelve, and in good shape. I didn't work out at that age, but I was thin and could run hard if I had to. You had to hold your breath most of the way up Stinky Steps, though. It was not like dead-body bad, which is something I know well now, but it was close. The Pigeon Man was out of his shack and feeding his caged pigeons. He was far enough away that we weren't worried, but he did look our way and I'm sure kept his eyes on us until we got to the top.

We walked to the left between a couple of apartment buildings and crossed narrow streets to Hamra. It was one of Beirut's main streets for shopping and eating. They drove their cars fast. Pedestrians walked slow. Not a care in the world. That's what it seemed. There were traditionally dressed Muslim men and women wearing headscarves. There were modern women wearing tight jeans, shorts, and even miniskirts. Roddy looked at them with full eyes. I never did. I was a late bloomer. Not always fun because I lost a lot of friends to girls, including Roddy.

As we weaved between small groups of people I noticed

a big black sedan pull to the curb in front of a café with outside seating. Two large men wearing dark suits and sunglasses stepped out of the front doors at the same time. A few seconds later, a third man stepped out of the rear driver's-side door, let another vehicle pass, then walked around to the rear door of the passenger side.

I nudged Roddy.

"Those guys look like Lebanese FBI or something," I said.

"I don't know."

The third man opened the rear door and a small older man with a thin grayish beard, dressed in fatigues and a keffiyeh, got out.

"That guy is someone important, though," Roddy added.

As we approached to pass, another man who was also wearing a keffiyeh, but with a thick black beard and large square-rimmed glasses and dressed in white pants and a white shirt, greeted the important guy with a kiss on each cheek. We walked around them, but I looked back as the two men sat at one of the café tables. They were given immediate service. The waiter bowed in respect to the older man. The three large men stood back, but not so far back they couldn't get to him if they needed to.

That memory always stood out to me. Even at twelve years old I knew something was hinky about them.

A clean-shaven, always-smiling Lebanese man worked the register behind the counter, while two younger men who looked like family members prepared the food. There were about six people ahead of us. That was not considered busy; usually there was a line out to the sidewalk. It was a popular spot for both locals and tourists, mostly because of the distinctive Lebanese pizza, which was topped heavy with ripe olives and feta cheese. That day, we both had a craving for a shawarma. Always messy, but always delicious.

They were efficient so it didn't take long for our turn. The clean-shaven man shot us a larger smile.

"My favorite American customers," he said with a thick accent. "Will it be the usual?"

"Yes, sir," Roddy said.

I nodded in agreement. He turned, told one of the younger men the order in Arabic.

"*Shukraan*," I said.

"*Shukraan*," Roddy repeated.

We both stood aside to let the next customer move up to the counter.

The young man preparing the food shaved the lamb from a rotating vertical rotisserie onto pita bread, then topped it high with hummus, tahini, vegetables, and ingredients I will never know. The rapid-fire assembling of the sandwich was like a dance. When they were done, we paid him, and he handed them to us without bagging them, knowing how we rolled—slamming them down while walking and always finishing before we got back to Stinky Steps.

We stood at the top of the hill with a view of the sea.

"You want to go snorkeling tomorrow?" I asked with my mouth full.

"Yeah, man."

"Looks clear down there," I said, referring to the Toufique danger. Just a few village kids taking advantage of the play-ground because most of the families from the building had not returned from summer vacation yet. That would be soon, though. Roddy talked about the other Americans. A few of them were girls, our age, and older teenagers. One was a "silly" kid he said I wouldn't want to hang out with. *Silly* meant *nerd*. The other, a kid named Lenny Beckham, was our age but looked older because he was big, so someone we needed around. He was the only young American Toufique feared. No rocks would be thrown with him by our side.

I looked toward the fort from the direction the rocks had been thrown.

"This is a good vantage point," I said. "From here, it doesn't look like the fort coulda been compromised from where the rocks were being thrown."

Roddy scanned the area, nodded while chewing.

ELEVEN

Finding sleep after a good day of goofing around was usually easy, but my parents were fighting, and my eyes wouldn't close. I listened, their voices muffled through the bedroom's closed door. Sounded like they were in the living room. My mother was the angry one. She had an unpleasant tone, but it was the occasional shrill that made me grind my teeth.

Buster was crowding my feet at the end of the bed. I gently kicked at him, got out of bed, and moved to the door. I opened it slowly, careful not to make any noise. I poked my head out and looked across the hall to the arched opening that revealed a tiny portion of the living room. Her voice louder now.

"...and why on earth did you agree to this godforsaken place? I hated the thought of India, but that would have been better than here. What am I to do?"

"Stay, boy," I whispered to Buster.

I stepped out, quietly closed the door behind me so Buster wouldn't follow, and walked with careful steps along the hallway, bent down, and creeped my way past the archway. I noticed Micheline's bedroom door was closed and my parents were sitting on the living-room sofa to the left of her room, facing the balcony. I wondered what Micheline was thinking. If it was loud enough for me to wake up, I couldn't imagine what it was like for her in that tiny room between the kitchen and the living room. Tommy? Hell, he could sleep through a war.

I sat on the floor to the side of the archway, where I could see the front door and my dad's light brown satchel on the other side, but close to me. I never noticed before, but it had a zipper at the side that was facing my direction. It zipped from the top where the flap folded over to the front, down to the bottom of the satchel.

"I feel so alone here," she continued.

I leaned against the wall to listen.

"I thought you were friends with Mrs. Stankey."

"Her first name is Joanne," she informed him.

"Joanne. And most of the American families will be returning from vacation soon. Some of them live in this building. I'm sure you'll make friends. I don't know why this is an argument."

"Argument? I'm lonely because you work these insane hours, sometimes don't even come home for a couple of days, and you call this an argument?"

"Your tone clearly suggests that it is."

"My tone? I'll try hard to work on my tone, maybe throw in an occasional smile."

Dad was silent.

"And what about Tommy? He has no one to play with. Micheline is the only friend he has. Graham doesn't give him the time of day."

That pissed me off. I wanted to jump in, but the truth was they were right. He was my little brother—what was I going to do with him? Not to mention he was a snitch. I wouldn't be able to get away with anything because it'd go straight to *Mommy.*

"That's how big brothers are," my dad said in my defense. "Like I said, I'm sure that he'll meet plenty of kids his age once school starts."

My attention turned back to the satchel and the zipper. My parents became like those unseen grownups in *Peanuts*—their words meant nothing. I turned and bent down so my right shoulder was resting on the carpet, then slid closer to the satchel. I don't know why, now. It was like it was supposed to be a secret zipper because I'd never noticed it before when Dad was carrying the satchel. It was concealed well, until now. That made me curious.

I knew it was wrong, but still I inched my hand toward the top and slowly unzipped it. He raised his tone. I rarely heard him get angry. I jerked my hand back and listened to make sure neither of them got up. No. The argument continued. I returned my attention to the zipper, but this time unzipped it all the way. Nothing was made visible. I'd have to stick my hand in there and hope that he didn't put some anti-spying device in there. I did, and soon felt what I thought was a handgun's grip. Dad let me shoot a pellet pistol once when we were back in the States. It felt a bit the same. I wrapped my hand around it. Couldn't get it all the way around, though. My hand wasn't large enough. It scared me, holding it, but at the same time excited me. I pulled at it, but not so hard that it'd make noise. It moved only slightly. There was something holding it in place. I felt around, my hand found a strap with a button. Of course, I unsnapped it, returned my hand to the grip. Pulled again. This time it released.

I had never seen a real gun. This one was something else. It looked like the ones I had seen pictures of in detective comic books, but this was the real deal. Blue steel, and what I learned soon after, a Smith & Wesson .38 police special. *Why did my dad have this? Was he a spy? Some sort of agent for the FBI?* I could not fathom any other reason for him to carry a gun, especially one that he had secreted in a hidden compartment of his bag.

I held it and examined it. I knew better than to look down the barrel; somehow I knew that was like inviting it to discharge a round. I held it sideways, looked at the hammer, trigger, the barrel that had some wear on it. *Had he ever shot someone with it?* My mind was racing. I pointed it down the hall, and for some reason, even though I knew it was like looking down the barrel, or maybe worse, I cocked the hammer back.

"Put the gun down, Graham," my dad said.

I turned. He had appeared out of nowhere—and fortunately before my finger went to the trigger, because I might have accidentally pulled it. He must have known that. That's why his voice was so calm. I obeyed. He picked it up, made the weapon safe again by slowly releasing the hammer.

"What the hell are you doing?" His tone was firm.

There was nothing I could say.

"Stand up," he demanded.

I obeyed, but with a reluctance that came with fear. He grabbed me by the front of my pajamas, almost pulled me up to the tips of my toes.

"Answer me."

My mother appeared behind him, on the other side of the archway. She was holding a martini glass, looked at my dad holding the pistol.

"Oh my God," my mother said. "What the hell are you doing?"

He released his grip. I stood straight again.

"It must have fallen out of the satchel," he said, but I didn't think he was covering for me, just preventing further argument. "Would you please sit down and let me take care of this?"

"Take care of what? Why were you grabbing him like that?"

"It's a misunderstanding. Please, let me handle this."

My mother huffed, sipped her drink once more, turned and walked back and plopped down on the sofa.

"Answer me, Graham."

"You were fighting," I said.

"What?" he asked, confused. "What does that have to do with anything? Adults fight, Graham. What does that have to do with you taking this out of my personal property?"

He showed me the pistol for emphasis.

I could smell the strong peaty odor of scotch on his breath. It was unpleasant.

"I don't know."

"You don't know? You damn well could have killed yourself or shot through a wall and killed Tommy. You'd better tell me what was in your head."

"It wasn't pointed toward Tommy's room."

"Don't get smart with me."

"I'm not."

"Answer me."

"I don't know," I said, and broke away from his grip, tearing a button off my pajama top, and ran to my bedroom and shut the door behind me.

I fell to the bed, grabbed Buster around the neck for comfort. *Stupid—stupid!* I said to myself.

Buster started snoring. My dad opened the door. I could see him in my peripheral vision but didn't turn to him.

"I am so disappointed in you. We'll talk about this tomorrow. You're grounded."

You know it's bad when you're grounded but not told for how long.

TWELVE

A day of snorkeling around the reefs was something I was looking forward to, but foolish curiosity kicked that out the door, closed it, and locked it after. I stayed in bed for a while and thought about snorkeling, though—how I loved getting out there to explore. My dad had gone with me and Roddy the first time so he could make sure it was safe, even though Roddy had already been out there several times over the past couple of years.

We walked to the Riviera Hotel and down to the tunnel that led under the Corniche to a saltwater pool, packed with sunbathers and little kids splashing around. The younger women and some of the older ones wore hardly anything at all: bikini bottoms that got lost between the cheeks of their asses. It was a tough place for preteens to be, especially Roddy. I'd have to smack him on the back of the head most of the time to keep him focused. We crossed the pool area to a cement wall that surrounded it. The wall was about eight feet in height and had a railing all around. Where the wall met the Corniche's seawall was our destination. We shouldered our gear contained in mesh bags, climbed over the rail, scaled down a bit, and grabbed the cement wall stretching down as far as we could, then dropped. Dad followed. After he made sure it was safe and I was strong enough to swim the reefs, he left us on our own. He was often about rules, but rarely stood in the way of my childhood adventures—unless, of course, they were foolhardy. There was something unspoiled about that time.

The old fisherman with his long bamboo pole was always two reefs over from where we swam. Our swimming spot was surrounded by sharp reefs, with only one narrow opening to the open sea. That kept the bigger fish out, except for a large grouper that managed to find its way in on my third time out. It was on the other side of a sandbar, but close enough that Roddy and I swam the hell out of there. It was big enough to swallow my leg, and far too big for the speargun.

There was another day when Roddy speared an octopus. Couldn't get it off the spear. Its flesh gripped the shaft, pulling itself up to the cord. Roddy swam to the reef and pulled it up. The old fisherman noticed, quickly secured his pole, and made his way to our reef. He was excited. He said something in Arabic.

"American," I said.

He made simple motions suggesting he could help. Roddy handed over the speargun and he removed the octopus like an expert, passed the speargun back to Roddy and spoke again, offering the octopus back. Roddy shook his head. "For you," he said, motioning his hands toward the man.

That day, the old fisherman became forever a friend. Over time, we speared eels for him, more octopus, and even shared some of our fish. He taught us how to get sea urchins off the reef wall and hold them so they tickled our palms with their poisonous spines, and how they were not a threat if the urchin was off the reef. The fisherman cut through the mouth of one of them to the orangey meat, ate it with a callused index finger, and offered us some, but we politely declined. Learned a lot from that old man. He was always there, but I wouldn't see him that day. Grounded. The first of many to come.

My dad knocked on the door.

"I'm up," I said.

He entered, said, "Get dressed. Take Buster out and come back for breakfast, then we're going for a drive."

Like reading an itinerary. He'd scheduled my day for me. I figured it had to do with my punishment.

"A drive? Where?"

"Graham, get dressed."

Dad had a red convertible hardtop Alfa Romeo. No diplomatic plates. He wanted to blend in, not attract attention.

It was a nice drive to the rugged mountains east of Beirut. All of them seemed connected, some with higher crests than others, with spotted areas of snow.

"Syria is on the other side of those mountains," he told me.

We parked behind a black four-door sedan, off a small dirt road below a slight incline with large rocks and a few tall cedar trees. He opened the trunk, pulled out his army-issued rucksack, and shouldered it.

A man stepped out of the driver's side of the sedan. He looked to be about my dad's age, was clean-shaven and wore dark slacks and a camouflage jacket over a white button-down shirt. Dad turned to him as he approached. They shook hands.

"*SabāH lḰér,*" Dad said like an American who is still learning.

"*SabāH nnūr,*" the other replied.

"This is my son, Graham. Graham, this is Alem."

"*MarHabā,*" I said.

"Very good pronunciation." The man smiled as he extended his hand.

We shook. His grip was firm.

"Let's go for a walk," Dad said to me.

Alem led the way. I didn't understand. I know that Dad liked to hike and explore. I figured this was something he had already set up with Alem before I was grounded and that he was a guide of some sort or worked at the embassy with him.

"Where are we going?"

"For a short walk along the mountainside," was all Dad said.

"It is not far from here," Alem said.

I knew better than to hound him. Last thing I wanted to do was extend the time I was grounded for. After about fifteen minutes we arrived at an area where the mountain was not so steep and mostly dirt and rock, with only a bit of vegetation. A couple of nice-sized lizards scurried from a boulder ahead of us. I wanted to lift the rock they went under.

"There a lot of scorpions here?" I asked Alem.

"Oh yes. You do not want to take your shoes off." He smiled again.

There was a small area that had a steep dirt incline. We stopped about twenty yards below that. I noticed spent shell casings on the ground and between the rocks ahead of me. I saw shards of glass at the bottom of the dirt incline and a few large and small empty cans with Arabic writing on them.

"Someone's been shooting here," I said pointing to the area where the casings were.

"No one lives around here, so folks sometimes shoot toward the steep incline at bottles and cans."

"It is safe," Alem said.

Dad pulled off his rucksack, set it on the ground.

"You want some water?" he asked as he pulled a green canteen from a side pocket.

"I guess."

He handed it to me. After I drank Dad offered it to Alem, but the man politely declined. Dad took a swig and returned the canteen to the pocket. He opened the top of the pack, reached in, and to my great surprise pulled out a small box of ammunition. It said .45 *caliber* on the side of the box. He put it on the ground, reached back into the rucksack, and pulled out a wooden box with a handle and two latches. He set the box on a level area beside the ammo, opened it. It was a pistol, but nothing like the .38. I had seen guns like that in my comics. I hoped he wasn't going to teach me a lesson by shooting me. For a split second my imagination got the best of me and the thought crossed my mind.

"This is my Colt .45. It was my service weapon in the Korean War. You're not ready for this one yet," Dad said.

He reached back in the rucksack and pulled out the .38. It was in a brown leather holster.

"We'll see if you're ready for this one."

I was going to shoot. *Damn.* I was certain of it. Grounded, and my punishment was going to the mountains and shooting a real gun. He removed the .38 from the holster, set the holster on the ground, released the cylinder, and took out the live rounds. Placed the live rounds in his right front pants pocket. Closed the cylinder, cocked the hammer and pointed it downrange. He dry-fired it.

"I will get cans," Alem advised my dad.

He set four cans along a flat area of the incline. They already had what I assumed were several bullet holes in them. Alem returned and stood a few feet behind my dad.

"Come over here," Dad told me.

My adrenaline kicked in. It was a nervous good feeling.

He handed me the gun, barrel pointed down. I took it by the grip, and my index finger immediately found the trigger.

"Take your finger off the trigger," he said, his tone stern. "Point the gun toward a can."

I obeyed. He stepped up to me and corrected my grip.

"Like this."

My hand was tense.

"Relax, Graham."

He showed me how to hold it.

"Now squeeze the grip like you want to break it."

I did.

"Point it downrange at one of the cans, and when you're ready to fire put your finger on the trigger. Take a deep breath, then exhale and pull the trigger."

That was old-school training, but how I learned. I did what he asked and pulled at the trigger, but it was like it was fighting me.

"It has a tough pull."

It finally clicked, but I expected it to be loaded so I jerked a bit and almost dropped the gun.

"Breathe."

I took a few deep breaths.

"Breathe normal, son. I don't want you passing out so I have to carry you back."

"I can carry the boy," Alem teased.

"I won't pass out."

"Okay. Now do the same thing but cock the hammer back first. Use your right eye to look through the middle of the rear sight until the front sight is aligned with a can. It's okay if the front sight looks a little blurry. Pull the trigger when ready."

I did. It was easier that time.

"That was good. There was less of a pull when the hammer was cocked, right?"

"Yeah."

"Okay, now do it ten more times."

"You're not going to put bullets in it?"

"How about I holster the weapon and we return home, or maybe you'll just do what I say."

I counted after each time I pulled the trigger, until I got to ten.

"With your finger off the trigger and the barrel pointed at the ground and away from my body, hand it over."

I did what he asked. He dropped the cylinder open, reached into his pocket, and pulled out a single round. He slid it into the cylinder, turned the cylinder so it would match up with the firing pin, and closed it.

"You keep that finger off the trigger. Understood?"

"Yes."

He moved behind me and said, "Now grip it like you mean business and point it at the can. Take your time."

I got one of the cans in my sight, cocked the hammer back and pulled the trigger. I forgot everything else. The recoil threw me back, the gun flying out of my hand. The force of it knocked my right hand back, hitting me hard on the lower lip. I felt my dad grab me from behind before my butt hit the rocky ground. He straightened me up. I tasted a little blood.

"Are you okay?"

"Damn," I said. And understood why he'd put only one live round in the cylinder.

Dad had another gun tucked away.

"This was my Army training pistol," he said. "It's a High Standard .22 pistol."

He released the magazine from the butt of the grip. It was empty. He loaded it with one .22 caliber round, slipped the magazine back in, and racked the slide to chamber a round.

Before he handed it to me, he said, "This is ready to fire. You be sure to keep the gun pointed toward the cans and your finger off the trigger or you're done. Understand?"

"Yes."

He handed me the gun and stood behind me again.

"Grip it like I told you. Like you mean business. Finger off the trigger. Get your eye lined up with the front sight like before."

I was hesitant. Last thing I wanted was to get smacked on the lip again.

"Take your time."

I placed my finger on the trigger, slowly squeezed, and surprised myself when it fired. I didn't drop the gun. It didn't have the kick the .38 had.

The can I was aiming at flew up a couple of feet and spun around and fell to the ground.

"Excellent," Dad said. "You're a natural."

It felt good. It did. He loaded it with a few more rounds, and sure enough, I hit every can.

"Damn natural, son." Dad smiled.

THIRTEEN

On the drive back, I held a handkerchief against my lip, checking it occasionally for blood. The early-afternoon sun was sharp on the eyes. Dad was wearing his aviator sunglasses.

I removed the handkerchief. The bleeding had stopped, but my lip felt a bit fat.

"Why do you have to carry a gun?" I asked.

"I don't have to carry it, I just do."

"Why, though?"

"I'm used to having it around. It's like a habit."

"Are you a spy?"

He turned to me, laughed a short laugh. I rarely heard him laugh.

"A spy," was all he said, almost as if to himself.

When we returned, Buster and Tommy ran from his bedroom to greet us. Dad rubbed Tommy's head with the palm of his hand, messing up Tommy's hair. After that he patted Buster a couple of times on the head. Micheline stepped out of the kitchen, noticed my fat lip.

"Oh my, what has happened?"

"Oh, he just had a little sense knocked into him is all," Dad told her.

She looked confused. My dad looked like he didn't want to explain.

"Is my wife here?"

"She said to tell you she would be at the Phoenician with Mrs. Stankey, for lunch."

"The Phoenician Hotel. Well, at least she's getting out," he said with a slight smile.

"I can take care of that lip for you," she told me.

"I'm okay."

"And your friend William called," she told me.

"We were supposed to go snorkeling," I told her but looked at my dad after.

"You're still grounded," he said and walked into his bedroom with the rucksack.

I noticed for the first time that his satchel was no longer on the floor at the archway.

"Can I call him back?"

He turned to me and said, "It would be impolite if you didn't."

I used that as an excuse to ask, "When can I tell him I can go swimming?"

"Three days."

Grounded for three days. Not bad at all, I thought; based on the severity of what I did, I thought it'd be the rest of the summer. I figured he realized I'd learned my lesson. I had. That gun scared the hell out of me, but my dad was smart enough not to let fear get the best of me. That's why he let me shoot the .22. I called Roddy.

"I thought you wanted to go snorkeling?" was the first thing he said.

"I did, but I got myself grounded."

"Crap, for what?"

"Being stupid."

FOURTEEN

My parents left for a party early that evening. Another American family back from the States, but it was adults only even though they had kids. I hoped that it was Lenny's family. Roddy spoke highly of him and I couldn't wait to meet him, even take him to the fort. Three could fit in there, but that's about it. It would also be nice to have strong backup. Toufique was less likely to act up around Lenny.

Micheline was in her bedroom. I was sitting on the floor listening to Jethro Tull's *Aqualung*. I had bought it at a record store in DC with Dad. Despite being tone-deaf, he did love music, mostly opera and jazz. He encouraged me to listen. Didn't matter if it was rock or what was considered alternative in those days, like Can and Velvet Underground. I'd like to think I had good taste in music for a kid my age. I took advantage of my parents' absence and played the music loud. Micheline wouldn't complain, and I didn't care if Tommy did.

I didn't hear him when he entered my room. He startled me.

"What're you doing?" I blurted.

"Can I have Buster in my room with me?"

"You scared again or something?"

"I just want to play with him."

I knew he was scared. He always got scared when my mother wasn't home. She coddled him.

I didn't want him hounding me, so I said, "I don't care." Then, to Buster: "Go on, boy." As if he'd listen to me.

Tommy had to take him by the collar and pull him off the bed. He looked back at me with big, baleful eyes as if he was being led out the door for punishment.

"C'mon, Buster," Tommy said.

I got lost in the music and made up a war adventure to roll with in my head. It was a good one. I got myself lost until the static sound of the record player's stylus signaled the end of Side One. I got up and turned it over, went to look out the window. Lights were on in the apartment buildings up the hill. I thought about getting the binoculars out but instead decided to walk toward the kitchen for a snack.

Micheline's door was open a bit, but not enough for her to notice I was there. I looked in as I passed, saw that she was sitting on the edge of her bed, feet on the area carpet. She had a nightgown on. It revealed her legs to the thighs.

She squeezed oil from a container onto the palm of her right hand, rubbed her palms together, and spread the oil on her right leg, starting at her calf. She repeated the process several times until she reached the top of her thigh. It was something to watch. I had never seen her do that before, and it stirred my insides in a way I had never experienced. Her legs were long and defined. The oil enhanced her skin to a perfect sheen. She lifted her left leg up to do the same thing. Her gown rode up enough to reveal the tight, beige-colored underwear that hugged her crotch. Something else in me began to stir, different this time. I could tell something weird was happening with my penis. I noticed a bulge in my pajama bottoms where my penis was, like it got bigger. It almost poked out. I didn't know what to think. Something wasn't right inside. I grabbed my crotch area to conceal it, ran to the bathroom next to my bedroom, and locked the door.

"What . . . ?" I whispered.

I took my hand away, was scared at first, but pulled my underwear and pants down to see what had happened.

My penis sprung out on me. It grew. It was swollen. It felt funny. It didn't hurt, though, and it sort of felt good. I was still scared. What happened? I didn't know how to fix it.

I looked at it in the mirror and was startled at the sight. Then it started to shrink again, until it was almost back to its normal size. I held it between two fingers so that I could examine it. It looked fine. The skin didn't break open and there was no blood or pain. I sat on the toilet, cradling my head, but my mind went back to her beautiful, oiled legs. It started to get hard again.

"Stop," I said a little too loud.

I didn't know what to think, except there was a possible connection between my penis and Micheline's legs. I did know it was something I would keep to myself, and the image of her legs was something I had to try to keep out of my head.

My parents were arguing when they came home. The argument was muffled by the bedroom wall and closed door. I looked at the clock on my nightstand. A little after 2300 hours. Military time. My father taught me. I liked to use it when I could. They weren't loud, but I was, always have been, a light sleeper. I heard a door slam. I was able to find sleep shortly after.

FIFTEEN

If Charlie Brown toughened up and had more hair and a crew cut, he would've looked like Lenny Beckham. I was pretty sure the only reason he wasn't nicknamed Charlie Brown was because he'd knock anyone's block off if they called him that. I met him the day I was released from being grounded. At the playground with Roddy. Swinging as high as we could and jumping off. Landing on the soft red sand. Getting the sand caught between my toes because I was wearing flip-flops. We gathered by the tetherball after we had had enough swinging and jumping. Lenny tossed us a couple more Tootsie Rolls from his pants pocket. After being in the States for most of the summer, he was well supplied. Didn't even make us pay for them. Everyone else yes, but not us. I was happy to be accepted by him.

The Tootsie Rolls were a bit squished from being in his pocket, but that didn't matter. I let it rest in my mouth before I chewed. Slowly.

"Let's see how close we can get to the Pigeon Man before he sees us," Lenny said.

I didn't think that was a good idea but didn't say anything.

"He'll chop our arms off if he catches us," Roddy said.

"Then don't let him catch you. C'mon, we done it before."

"Yeah—and between him, the vipers, and scorpions, we barely made it out alive."

"Three Tootsie Rolls for the one who gets closest."

Roddy looked at me like he expected me to make the decision.

"I think you gotta raise the ante," I told Lenny.

"Huh?"

"Like poker. Need more than three in the pot to make it worth it."

"Damn, the new kid's good."

Roddy chuckled.

"Three Tootsie Rolls and a Snickers."

That was hard to refuse, but I was still worried about it. Roddy and I didn't play games like that. I wondered if Lenny was testing me.

"I'm in," I said.

The Pigeon Man was at his spot on the hill, but the pigeons were not out. We could see him from the playground, wearing a white robe. Looked like he was sitting on a chair, staring out over the buildings toward the sea.

We had already talked to Lenny about the fort, and that it had to stay between us. Lenny swore to keep it to himself. Roddy discreetly pointed it out to him as we passed it, along the bottom of the hill following the wall. There was a large ficus tree and clumps of thick vegetation along that side of the hill toward his shack. Made for good concealment, but not so thick you couldn't run if you had to.

Lenny was leading. He stopped on the other side of the

ficus, looked up the hill. I looked up in the same direction. Couldn't see the shack. Roddy and I were wearing flip-flops and I did not think it was a good idea. I could tell by his face he didn't either. Lenny wore Converse sneakers with no socks. We all had shorts on, and short-sleeved T-shirts.

"All right, men. Onward," Lenny said.

A bit too sure of himself, I thought.

We crouched down and slowly walked up the side of the hill, taking cover behind bushes along the way. Before long we could see the side of the shack, but not the Pigeon Man. It was about one hundred yards up the hill and to our left.

"I'm the judge," Lenny whispered. "So I'll watch from here."

"What?" I questioned.

"It's between you two. You can't expect me to be a part of it and probably winning. I'm the one offering the prize."

"That's not fair," Roddy said.

"One of you is going to win. Who'll it be?"

I bent down, started walking toward the shack.

I heard Roddy mumble, "Crap."

About twenty yards out we stopped and hid behind a tall thicket. I noticed Roddy's ankles were scratched up, but not dripping blood. Mine were too.

"We can stop here and call it a tie."

"Or we can both go on and touch the side of the shack and call it a tie," I said, wanting to impress my new friend. Let him know I wasn't scared.

"Dang, Graham, we're gonna get ourselves chopped up."

"We're faster than that old man."

"You think that until he whacks your arm off with a machete."

"Shh. He'll hear us. C'mon."

I looked at Roddy, trying to urge him along. I knew I wouldn't go without him.

He tightened his lips, crawled out from the thicket. I followed, making sure to stay by his side.

"Same time," I told him.

He nodded.

We crawled the rest of the way, careful not to stumble over a rock and disturb any vipers or scorpions. Somehow, we made it to the side of the shack. The Pigeon Man had to be on the other side, and hopefully still sitting down. We stood up. Heard scuffling to our left toward the front of the shack. Sounded like someone walking. We knew it was him. No more noise. We turned. I knew Roddy thought about running. I did too. But if it wasn't the Pigeon Man, our running away would get his attention and he'd more than likely recognize us from the building or something. More noise and then a man speaking out in Arabic, like it was a question. The voice was stern. Strong, but not loud.

Roddy ran. I froze, but only for a split second. I knew we were making too much noise, but looking behind us was out of the question because we'd lose our balance and tumble down the steep part of the hill. Maybe die. That's what I thought at the time. Lenny was farther down the hill, looking up. It didn't take him long to turn and run too. He was a big kid, but faster than hell. He got to the bottom of the hill and the ficus tree long before us, but he didn't stop there. By the time we got down the hill, Lenny was gone. We hid behind the ficus, and after a moment I peeked out. The Pigeon Man never came after us. I saw him up there, machete in his right hand, holding it against his hip and leg. He knew where we were. It was obvious. He stood there still and ominous, like a character out of a Grimm fairy tale. That was the second time in my life I felt like I was going to get killed. There would be other times, though. The third would come soon.

SIXTEEN

Lenny realized that the only fair thing to do—and the only way to save face after leaving us behind—was to even up the winnings. Roddy and I each got three Tootsie Rolls and a Snickers bar. We ate some of them in the lot behind the apartments, sitting on the low wall that dropped at least ten feet on the other side to the vacant lot and demolished building. Lenny was chucking small rocks toward the white curtain hanging in the fallen archway, but not hitting it. Rock lizards scurried to safety from the tops of fallen cinder blocks. Our legs were scratched up; Lenny's, not so much. But I knew I'd have to explain. Not the way it really happened, though. *Hunting down lizards.* That's a good one. Simple and doesn't need further explanation, except that we didn't catch any.

We talked about the adventure, convinced ourselves the Pigeon Man hadn't seen our faces. Still, the possibility was there. We didn't talk about it. It was almost lunchtime. I saved the three Tootsie Rolls for later.

"I gotta get back for lunch," Lenny said. "Mom's gonna make grilled-cheese sandwiches."

"I should check in too," Roddy said.

"Yeah. Maybe see you guys later, then?" I said.

"Sounds good," Lenny said.

We snuck around to the front, making sure the Pigeon Man wasn't searching the area for us. It was clear. We took the stairs up to our apartments.

Buster never barked when I was unlocking the door. I was sure he sensed it was me and that we had a certain connection. I had to pull him off me. Always greeted me like he thought I was never going to return.

My mother was in the den listening to Leonard Cohen on the reel-to-reel. My parents had a large collection of records and Dad transferred most of them onto tape, so it'd be less of a hassle when it came time to move. I could smell the cigarette smoke wafting in from the den as I walked to the kitchen. Micheline was in there. Tommy was sitting at the kitchen dinette table eating a peanut butter and jelly sandwich. A large bowl of potato chips beside his plate.

"I can make you a sandwich. Peanut butter and jelly," Micheline said.

"Okay."

I tried not to look at her legs. Instead, I grabbed a handful of potato chips.

"Don't eat them all," Tommy said.

"You think you're going to eat them all?"

"Yes."

"You might need Mommy to protect you if you think I'm not going to take some."

"Stop," he whined.

"There are more, little boy," Micheline said with a comforting smile.

Her legs. Damn, her legs. Also, the sundress she wore. It

revealed some cleavage. All those thoughts. Dad never had The Talk with me, so I didn't know what was going on.

I ate my sandwich and bowl of potato chips in the bedroom, tossed a couple of chips to Buster, one after the other. He caught them in the air like a champ, begged for more.

"Back off," I told him.

He sat. Ears perked, but not all the way. The tips of his ears bent over.

I went to the balcony, sat on a chair, ate the rest of my lunch while checking the hill out. The Pigeon Man was gone, or maybe in the little shack, or maybe searching for us.

The rest of that day was spent in the fort with Roddy and Lenny. I was wearing sneakers this time, and a different shirt. So was Roddy. We wanted to minimize the possibility of the Pigeon Man recognizing us. We walked the wall to the fort, trying not to look suspicious. The fort was well concealed. We all managed to squeeze in. Lenny loved it, especially peering through the binoculars at the kids in the playground, and at the village.

That was how we spent most of our remaining summer days, as well as going snorkeling—an activity Lenny did not like because he didn't enjoy swimming. That's what he said. I thought he was afraid of the sea. I never teased him about that. He'd knock my head off, or wrestle me to the ground and grind my face in the dirt. He did that more than once. Trying to teach me wrestling moves. He made the junior wrestling team in sixth grade. He was good. His healthy weight coupled with his strength made him dangerous.

Micheline often fried the fish I caught on those summer days. This time there were four, about three pounds each, looked like freshwater sunfish. We had them for dinner. Dad was always impressed with my bounty, how I got them myself and how Micheline fried them up. I think they reminded him of his childhood. He was an outdoorsman. Grew up on a potato farm in Northern Minnesota. There was a nearby lake. He loved to fish, hunt, and camp.

When he came to my bedroom later to say goodnight, he said, "We're going camping next weekend with Mr. Beckham and his son, Leonard. You met him yet?"

"Yes. Lenny. He's a new friend."

I figured he had planned it after the fish dinner and called Mr. Beckham. They worked together at the embassy.

"Good. You can invite your other friend Bill, too, if you'd like."

"Do you know his dad too?"

"I've run into him a few times. Nice man."

"Is Tommy going?"

"No. Just you older boys."

"Cool."

"'Night."

"Goodnight."

He turned the light off and shut the door behind him. It didn't take long for Buster to start snoring. It was an odd, comforting sound.

I wondered if Dad would bring guns so we could shoot.

SEVENTEEN

Mr. Beckham looked to be about my dad's age. A bit taller, heavier, and with a military cut. An older Lenny. He carried himself like he was in the military. I wondered if he was one of the Marines there, or if he wore regular clothes, like Dad did.

It took a little more than two hours to take the old train with rickety wooden benches from Beirut to a small village in Southern Lebanon. A dozen or so other men, women, and a couple of young kids were sitting in the train for most of the trip. A musty, human smell was caught in the dry air, like it had always been there. It would stick to your clothing and stay with you for a while.

Mr. Beckham and my dad sat together. Alem sat alone a couple of rows ahead of me and Roddy. Lenny had a bench opposite ours, his backpack next to him. Our packs were tucked above us on racks. Lebanon was a mountainous country, not so visible looking out the window to the west. Lenny's window revealed more of the peaked mountains and rocky terrain. I thought about what my dad had said, that Syria, another country, lay on the other side of those mountains and Israel was to the south. *Was that my mother's homeland because she was Jewish?* How close would we be to the border of Israel?

I was quiet most of the way, daydreaming of running away from the campsite to Israel and joining the army there. I'd read somewhere that the Israelis had the best military force in the world. Aside from the United States, of course. It was a small country surrounded by enemies, and one that was created not so long ago. How could they come so far so fast? I thought maybe it was where I belonged. Not like I was unhappy at home or really did want to run away. Just a boy's daydream.

From the tiny train station, we hiked to a river that Alem told us opened to the Mediterranean Sea to the west. It was an old river. We hiked east along the river's bank for about an hour, until it narrowed enough that we could cross to the other side.

"There," Alem said while he pointed.

Steep rock cliffs and large old trees on the other side of the river. There were several cliff overhangs, and an open area that looked like a good campsite. There was also a large rock overhang on the bank of the river, where its current slowed around the bend to make a good swimming hole.

Though we'd brought bathing suits, I had second thoughts as we crossed the river on a series of big, loose rocks. The water was ice-cold, and the swimming hole was so dark—so deep—that you couldn't make out the bottom. First thing Alem and Mr. Beckham did after we crossed and set our packs on open ground was find dry wood to make a campfire. Dad helped Lenny, Roddy, and then me set up our small tents. All of them in line next to each other.

The men returned with wood, and started a nice camp-fire near the water. It was still early afternoon and we were hungry. Dad was the one tasked with making our lunch. Simple peanut butter and jelly sandwiches and pita bread with hummus on the side. He had everything tucked in his army-green backpack. It was twice the size of his rucksack. I noticed a bottle of liquor in it. Something for the men. Looked like the scotch he drank at home. I was sitting with him in the den one early evening and told him it smelled funny, like wet ashes after a campfire had been extinguished. He teased me. Coaxed me over and grabbed me. He stuck his index finger in the glass. I knew what he was doing and tried to squirm my way out of his hold. He was laughing. I had my game face on. He managed to rub my lips and teeth with his index finger. I thought it was disgusting. Pretended to spit and vomit. He laughed more. Didn't realize then how much I'd end up loving scotch later in life.

The temperature was nice, not like in the city. Despite how cold the water felt, Roddy and I changed into our swimsuits. Lenny bowed out.

"I don't like swimming," he said.

We knew.

"My boy never was much of a swimmer," his dad said. "All that baby fat he's still carrying. You probably won't sink, just float downriver." He gave a crooked half-smile.

Lenny rolled his eyes toward us. He tried to play it like it was nothing, but we could tell. It wasn't funny because we were all scared.

We changed up behind our tents. I wore my under-wear under my swim trunks because I had always felt uncomfortable hanging loose. I packed smart and had spare underwear. Dad put up a clothesline that stretched from one tree to the other and was a few steps away from the fire. Guess he figured we'd get wet or our clothes dirty enough they'd have to be washed in the river.

Roddy was first to climb up the large rocks to the overhang. I followed but knew I wouldn't be the first to jump. It was about ten feet high. The water seemed impossibly deep, like a jump straight into a tunnel. I feared what might be down there. Swimming off the reefs, at least we had our flippers on. If something was going to nip you, it would get the flipper first. But nothing ever did nip at us. This was fresh water, so I knew there wouldn't be sharks or anything real big. I wanted to ask Alem to make sure, but at the same time didn't want to know.

Roddy leaped in. A nice cannonball. Good form, but he was lighter than me so the splash wasn't high.

"C-c-cold," he said like a stutter.

He sank back down and popped up.

"Getting used to it, though. C'mon."

I saw my dad at the bank near the hole. He had his camera to his eye, ready to snap pictures.

I jumped out. Landed in the water but didn't know how high my splash was. Honestly didn't even think about it, because I lost my breath as soon as I hit the ice-cold water. Thought I would drown but kicked and flopped my arms to the surface, where I took a deep breath.

"D-d-damn," I said, not thinking what my dad would think. "Cold, cold."

I shivered immediately and started swimming to the bank.

"You'll get used to it," Roddy assured me. "Seriously."

I stopped swimming when I could feel the rocky bottom with my toes.

"Lost my breath," I told him, but was looking at Dad.

"Just dunk down a couple of times. Feels good after a minute."

Dad seemed fine, even though he'd always been strict about swearing.

"Minute's too long," I said.

"You're fine," I heard Dad say.

I looked up at him. He was close to shore.

I dunked myself up and down a few times. I got used to it.

EIGHTEEN

Dad and Mr. Beckham brought several packages and small cans of what they called *Meal, Combat, Individual Rations.* Enough for all of us. That's what they were, but he said they still referred to them as *C Rations* because that's what they'd lived on during the Korean War. The three of us were excited about it. Felt like soldiers. We had meat with beans in a tomato sauce, warmed over the fire, and several chocolate-chip cookies. The cookies were a bit dry and crumbly but tasted fine. I don't know what the grownups were eating but it looked mostly like drinking to me, including Alem. The bottle of scotch that my dad brought. They sipped it from tin cups. Sat on large rocks but then moved to the other side of the campfire. We sat across from them on a long log. The officers and the grunts.

After eating, we found sticks and poked at the fire. It was getting dark. Lenny swatted at the rising sparks, sometimes tried to clap them in the palms of his hands.

"They're gonna bite ya," Mr. Beckham said.

Lenny looked at him darkly, then did it anyway.

"I used to slap bees," he told us. "Never got stung 'cause I did it so fast."

He clapped a large spark, tried to sound like Bruce Lee after.

The dark seemed to enfold the landscape. Clouds were high so the stars were not visible. The only light came from the fire. Alem and the dads finished half the bottle and were smoking cigars, caught up in a political conversation having to do with Israel and the PLO. I didn't understand at the time. Heard a lot of that kind of talk from Dad, though. We got into our own conversations, mostly embellished stories, like when Roddy and I had rocks thrown at us. The small bruises on our backs and legs became large, painful welts, and of course we barely made it out alive.

"It was definitely Toufique," Roddy said, even though we didn't know for sure.

"Maybe the Pigeon Man," Lenny said.

"No way," Roddy told him. "He's too tall. We woulda seen him poking his head up."

"Yeah," I agreed.

"Maybe you're right," Lenny said. "I've never seen him down from that shack of his. Wouldn't recognize him if he was. And you know, that's what makes him so dangerous."

"What do you mean?" I asked.

"He could be right behind you and you wouldn't know it. Catch you when you're somewhere all alone. One big swing"—Lenny swung his stick toward my head like a machete—"and that'd be it, like an Arab ninja. Who knows how many bodies he has buried on that hill?"

"That's what Roddy here said. I think it's all stories, though. He'd've been caught otherwise."

"You think so?" Lenny looked at me direct. His eyes again went stony, like a grown man's would.

"No, they'll just cut off your right hand, or worse," said Roddy, interrupting.

"You serious?" I asked.

"Heck ya. For real," Roddy said. "It's not like they have detectives here like in the States."

"And from what I've seen, it looks like the Pigeon Man still has both of his hands."

"Why the heck you challenge us to go up there if he's so dangerous? Trying to get us killed?"

"C'mon now," is all Lenny said.

I wanted to rag on him, but the moment felt weird, like I didn't know him well enough. I left it at that.

"What's the deal with Toufique?" I asked.

"We're Americans," Lenny said.

Roddy poked at the dying fire.

"Put a couple little logs on it," Mr. Beckham said.

Roddy and Lenny reached for some, dropped them over the fire. They crackled, then caught. The two backed away when the flames got a bit too high.

"Why would he hate Americans so much?"

"I guess 'cause we're not from his country. I don't know," Lenny said.

"My dad said they're not all like that," Roddy added.

"Like Alem," I said quietly so the adults wouldn't hear.

"Yeah," Roddy said. "It's mostly a religious thing, my dad said. Like we're heathens or something."

"Heathens." Lenny snickered. "Right. I'm gonna cut your hand off." He whacked the stick on Roddy's wrist.

"Ow." He rubbed his wrist. "That's what my dad says, anyway."

We could've stayed up all night, but Dad said we needed a

good night's sleep because we had to get up early. We grumbled, trying to convince them we'd be okay. Didn't work. The dads were adamant, so we said our goodnights and went to our tents.

I took my shoes off but kept my clothes on. You never knew. I think Alem was teasing, but he said we might hear the hyenas crying out in the night, but not to worry. How could there be hyenas here? This wasn't Africa.

I woke up later that night with a full bladder. Should've gone before bed. Not something I could hold until morning. I'd have to put my shoes on and brave the dark by myself. *Hyenas—that was a joke, right?* Thought about peeing in my canteen and accidentally losing it later but decided against it. It was an army canteen Dad had bought for me in DC, and the only one I had. I even used it at my bedside for when I got thirsty late at night. Can't piss in that. Nothing else here, either.

I grabbed the flashlight beside the sleeping bag, turned it on, and set it down so I could see while tying my shoes. I picked it back up and unzipped the tent. Stepped out, careful not to shine the light on the other tents. Thought about it. At least on Lenny's tent. Maybe he'd wake up and go with me. No. That was cowardly. Besides, I was sure that Alem was playing with us. *Hyenas.* What a joke.

I followed the craggy cliff a few feet until I reached a large tree. The tree on my right side and the cliff toward my back seemed like good protection, but I was nervous. Harder to piss when you're nervous. I did—a long, arcing surge of urine. Felt damn good.

The moon was almost full. It illuminated the trees across the river, where there was a small clearing. It was there that

I saw the shadowy figures of four men. Not wanting to be seen, I turned my flashlight off. I hurried my piss as best I could, thought about running to my dad's tent and waking him up. One of them lit a cigarette, though. It wasn't so far that I couldn't make out Mr. Beckham's face when the lighter flicked on. Two of the other men could have been Dad and Alem. Didn't know about the fourth man. I had to make sure if that was my dad or not. If it wasn't, I'd go wake him up.

The men were far enough away from where I was, and the tents, that they were hard to make out and hear. I wished that I had brought my binoculars so I could conduct surveillance from where I was. I had to get closer, at least to the river's edge. I zipped up my pants, tucked the flashlight in my back pocket, and snuck over to the overhanging rock, careful not to be seen or heard.

I crawled along the ledge to where my head was almost hanging over. That was where I had jumped into the river. The man beside Mr. Beckham lit a cigarette with a match. It was my dad. The moonlight, along with the match, made it obvious. Still couldn't make out the other two, but one of them had a long beard and looked to be dressed in fatigues. He was shouldering what appeared to be a machine gun. The magazine was long, and he tucked the weapon to his hip with his hand. He looked familiar—but then, to a kid like me, so many of the men with thick beards in that country looked familiar. They were speaking Arabic, but I couldn't understand the words. Even if I was close enough, I wouldn't know what they were talking about. Alem appeared to be translating for Dad and Mr. Beckham.

Mr. Beckham flicked his cigarette to the ground near his feet. Smooshed it out under his shoe. My dad did the same.

For a moment it was quiet. My dad placed his right hand on Alem's shoulder, then walked away with the man who carried the machine gun, disappearing into the woods. Mr. Beckham and Alem spoke for a few seconds, then turned to walk back toward the river crossing and the tents. I scurried off the rock and quietly, but as quick as I could, made my way back to my tent. Once inside, I zipped it up, took the flashlight from my pocket, and sat on the sleeping bag. I looked at my wristwatch. Past midnight.

I squirmed around on top of the sleeping bag until I found a comfortable position on my back. I thought about what my dad might be doing out there, and why he'd brought us along. For the first time, I didn't feel safe. It wasn't like the fear of hyenas, or a neighborhood bully, or what might nip my toes in the river. It was real.

NINETEEN

It was still dark out when I woke to the rain thumping hard against my tent. I looked at my Seiko Diver's wristwatch: 3 a.m. It was a hard rain. It was coming through the meshed opening at my tent. I zipped up. The clouds from the day before had cleared by nightfall to reveal the bright moon, so the storm must have come fast. The sound of the heavy rain pelting the tent somehow both enlivened me and lulled me. Scary and calming. I tucked myself back in the sleeping bag and tried to get lost in its rhythm.

Dad woke me. I checked the time again: 6 a.m. He was halfway inside my tent, soaking wet. It was still raining hard.

"Pack up everything as fast as you can. We have to get out of this storm," he said. Even though he tried otherwise, he sounded urgent and panicked. "Hurry up, now."

He left. I poked my head out, and damn if it didn't look like I had slid closer to the river, along with the other tents. I stuffed my belongings in the pack. I was wearing my clothes from the day before so didn't have to worry about getting dressed. I had a light jacket, not close to waterproof. I put it on anyway, dragged my pack with me as I stepped out of the tent.

The rain was streaming down from the cliffs around us, like waterfalls. The water on the ground was like a shallow rapid. Our tents had indeed slid about five feet. I must have slept hard not to feel it. I started taking down the tent. I saw Roddy, who was already packed, being directed by Lenny's dad to stand under a large overhang at the wall of a cliff, sheltered by the rain. His tent still up. Mr. Beckham ran to Lenny to help him pack quicker.

"Don't worry about the tent," my dad shouted to me.

"I can't leave my tent," I yelled back.

"Get with the boys in the sheltered area. Now."

I ran with my pack to join them. Didn't matter to me if I stayed in the rain. I was already soaked to my bones and didn't think I could get any wetter.

"Damn," Lenny whispered when I joined them.

Roddy ran up to us after. We tucked close together against the rock wall.

The river was raging, now flooding over the banks. The water level seemed to be rising by the second. Our swim trunks were no longer on the line. I figured they were somewhere downriver.

The tents were suddenly swept away by a gush of water like a wave. Taken by the river. Most of them turned to their sides, slapped against the rocky bank of a bend near the overhang.

"That's unreal," Roddy said.

"Oh man," was all I could say.

I was scared but tried not to show it. Dad, Mr. Beckham, and Alem joined us after they had gathered as much as they could. They couldn't squeeze all the way into the sheltered area with us, so—like true soldiers—they endured the soaking rain.

They took turns looking up the cliff in case something like a tree or a large log was swept over. All of them shielded their eyes from the rain with their hands like a salute.

"Can't cross the river when it's like this. Just have to wait it out," Mr. Beckham said.

Alem looked worried. He kept his eyes toward the top of the cliff.

"You boys are safe in there. Nice sheltered area there," my dad tried to comfort us.

"I think it's cool," said Roddy.

"I don't like to swim," Lenny countered.

"No one is going to have to swim," his father assured us. "Like Mr. Sanderson said, we'll wait it out, cross the river, and be home before you know it."

Before you know it. Can't count how many times I had heard that. Had it ever gone that way?

TWENTY

By 8 a.m. the rain had died down to a steady drizzle. There was an occasional downpour, like God wringing out a towel, but it didn't last. The river was still high and rapid. The adults were scouting the river's edge ahead of us for a safe place to cross. We were sitting on the log where the campfire used to be. Everything cleared. A fresh, new, muddy landscape. Water still streamed along the ground at our feet and into the river's swift current.

"Why can't we hike along this side of the river to the village?" Lenny asked in a loud voice.

"The river widens," Alem said. "It will be flooded."

"And it's higher ground on the other side," my dad added. "I think we're all wet enough. Don't you, boys?"

The river bent around the cliff in the other direction. The path on this side that went up the river and around the cliff was no longer there. Water covered it, all the way up to the bottom of the cliff. So, heading up the river was not a consideration. We had to cross here.

Dad and the other men looked like they had decided on a course of action. Alem walked to where the clothesline was tied from one tree to the other. He untied each end and wound up the cord. Dad and Mr. Beckham approached us.

"The river won't go down anytime soon," Dad said. "Wood is too wet to get a fire started, so trying to wait it out until tomorrow is out of the question. It'll get too cold by nightfall."

"You boys ready for an adventure?" Mr. Beckham asked.

"I'm not a good swimmer, Dad."

"I know, son. Current is too strong for that. The spot we're crossing at looks to be shallow, so you won't have to swim."

"No. No swimming allowed," Dad tried to joke. "Where we crossed before still seems to be the shallowest part. Let's go over a few things. Follow me."

We walked to the area where we crossed. The river was overflowing its banks. The boulders we had crossed on could not be seen and the current was heavy, so it was hard to judge how deep the water was. I had my doubts. I know Lenny did too. Roddy did not appear to be worried. He even had a slight smile.

"We'll cross here," Dad said. "It's a bit wider so shouldn't be deep. Alem will secure me with the line and I'll cross first to make sure the way is clear. The line is only a guide to follow, not to hold onto. It's not strong enough. The four of you will link arms and face upriver and cross step by step. Like slow crab steps. Mr. Beckham will be the anchor. Mr. Beckham and I have done this before. It'll be a piece of cake for you boys."

"When did you have to do something like this?" Roddy asked.

I thought that was a good question. Something I wanted to know because it'd make me feel better.

"During the war," Mr. Beckham said. "Korea and Vietnam."

"You and Mr. Beckham were soldiers together?" I asked my dad.

"No, but there were plenty of rivers to cross. Listen up, now. I want you to unstrap your packs at the hip."

We all did.

"You won't fall, but just in case you do, unshoulder the packs and let them go. The water will fill them up fast. Understood?"

We nodded.

"I have crossed this river many times," Alem said.

"When it was like this?" Lenny asked.

"Not especially, but close."

"Okay," Dad continued. "Alem, could you try to find three strong hiking sticks for us?"

"Yes."

"*Shukran*," Dad said. "Remember to let your packs go if you fall, boys."

"This should be fun," Roddy told me and Lenny.

"You think?" Lenny said with sarcasm and with a softer tone so his dad couldn't hear.

"You're the strongest one here, Lenny," I said—an effort to reassure him.

"Yeah, but my dad said I'm big-boned, so that's why I'm not a good swimmer. I sink like a stone."

"You heard my dad. It's shallow at this spot."

"Until you fall, and it drags you downriver."

"You fall, we all fall," I said. I felt like a soldier after saying it.

We looked at one another, nodded with assurance. A team. It was a good feeling, but that didn't mean I wasn't worried.

After a few minutes, Alem returned with two large sticks,

one of which he had to break in half. Mr. Beckham secured the line around dad's waist.

"You'll need the strong ones," Dad said, and grabbed one that was smaller in diameter. "Okay. Been a while since I had to do this. Keep the line taut."

"I got it," said Mr. Beckham.

Dad stepped into the water sideways and facing upriver. The water was over his knees. He slowly sidestepped, holding the stick with his left hand and poking it in the water for depth and potential obstacles. It didn't take him long to make it halfway. He prodded the next step with the stick. It was obviously deeper. He didn't show it, but I knew he was worried—more for us than himself, because he looked back toward us before he stepped. He sank to his waist, which would be like to my chest or shoulders. He almost lost his footing. He looked silly trying to regain himself. It was something uncomfortable for me to watch because it looked like weakness, and I had never imagined he could be weak.

"Slippery here," he advised loudly. His voice was hoarse.

I looked the other way. Didn't want to watch him if he slipped all the way. It'd be an image I'd never get out of my head.

When I looked back, he was almost to the other side.

"Almost there, Carl," Mr. Beckham called out.

Dad used the stick to balance himself as he stepped up to the other side, ankle-deep in the overflow. The original bank was not visible anymore. He regained his footing, untied the rope from his waist. He tied it to a large tree.

"Beck, secure the boys with the rope you have," Dad yelled.

"Roger that."

They were so calm, like this was nothing more than training.

Mr. Beckham took the rope that was lashed to the side of his backpack. It was a long rope—it looked stronger than the line across the river—but it wasn't long enough to use for that. He tied it around my waist first, then looped it and secured it around Roddy's waist, Lenny's, and finally his own. *If he goes down,* I thought, *we all go down.* Lenny's dad was a big guy. Even at twelve years old, I didn't think that was such a good idea.

"Okay now. Listen up. Alem will be the lead, followed by Graham, Bill, and you, Lenny. I'm the anchor. We all lock arms, face upriver and stay ahead of the line. That's our path. Questions?"

"Can I just stay on this side? Wait it out?"

"That's ridiculous, son," his dad told him. "Do you think I'd leave you here alone?"

"No. You can camp out on the other side."

"That's foolish talk. Now do what I say. Understood?"

"Yes, sir," he said with reluctance.

Everyone had a weakness. I learned that at an early age, maybe on that day. My dad. Lenny. Lenny's was his fear of drowning. He was never so afraid of the water that he wouldn't go near it or even in it. He just had to see the bottom and know he could touch. He was, in more ways than one, the rock on our team. The fact that, despite his fear, he still was able to move forward with what had to be done, made me feel better. I knew he was more frightened than I was.

"What if you slip?" I asked Mr. Beckham. "Won't you take us all with you?" I instantly regretted the question..

Think before you speak. That's what Dad always said. Save you a lot of grief.

"That's not going to happen, Graham," he told me.

I wasn't convinced, but he was the adult and had survived two wars, so I wasn't about to argue.

Alem stepped in, prodded the area to his side with the stick before he continued. My left arm was locked tight around his right arm and my right arm tight around Roddy's—who, strangely enough, still had that grin on his face.

TWENTY-ONE

I stepped into the river after Alem. The line secured across the river was high enough so it wouldn't trip us up if we slipped. The current was strong, but not strong enough to take my feet out from under me. I knew it would get stronger, though. Roddy stepped in, followed by Lenny and Mr. Beckham.

I heard Dad shouting, "You got this," a couple of times.

"Stay tight," Mr. Beckham said calmly, followed by, "Good job, boys" for additional assurance.

The water was cold. It slapped at my waist. Deeper than expected. Alem took slow, measured steps. I wanted him to speed up. I was looking upriver, trying to stay focused. I peeked toward the left, noticed we were more than halfway. It was deeper. I felt my way with my toes before taking the next side step. I tapped my toe against a large rock. Alem took a step, but I didn't. That messed up my balance. My fault, not Alem's.

Funny thing, because I thought to myself how worried I was that Mr. Beckham would take us down, and there I went. I panicked as I tried to steady myself. Ended up releasing my locked arm from Alem's. He tried to grab me. I heard loud voices, like commands. Roddy still had his arm locked to mine, trying to keep me up. I saw his face. Wasn't grinning. He was turned as I was taken down. Couldn't tell if he went down with me—or anyone else, for that matter. All I remember was having to fight to keep my head above water. I felt like a fishing bobber. I was slapping at the water with both hands. I knew I was still tied to Roddy because I felt it and I wasn't being taken down the river. I went under again, swallowed water and managed to get my head above the surface enough to cough, spit, see Alem struggling to reach me. I was taken under again. Roddy went down with me. I tried to reach for him and felt his head. I brought my hand down and grabbed the rope that secured us, trying to steady myself and stand, but that didn't work. I was sure that was it for me, and the last thing I'd see was Alem, a good man I barely knew. *What kind of thought was that?*

Next thing I knew, I was pulled up and out of the water. It was Alem and Dad. Roddy had gone under with me, but Lenny and his dad were now pulling him up.

That was the third time I thought death would come for me.

We made it to the other side. Lenny kissed the ground dramatically. I remembered the look on his face when my head bobbed out of the water. It was quick, but there he was, a fighter's face, standing strong, that rock-solid look in his eyes. And then like a kid again, kissing the ground and crying out, "Man, oh man."

Father hugged me after he and Mr. Beckham untied our line. That was the first and only time I remember him doing that. Getting emotional. Not even something he did after the car accident. It felt awkward.

"I tripped on a rock," I told him.

He let me go, looked at me and said, "Everyone made it across. I told you it'd be an adventure." He smiled.

I still wonder what we must've looked like sitting on those rickety wooden benches as the train made its way back to Beirut. Mud to our waists, clothes still mostly wet. The train was crowded. People stared. Lenny, Roddy, and I had to share a bench. Not a lot of room but I didn't care. Don't think they did either. We were just happy to be headed back home.

We were quiet for most of the train ride. All that excitement and the long hike back had taken a toll on us. I forgot about that final night of camping, when I saw my dad and the man with the machine gun walk off into the dark. When I remembered a week later, alone in the bathroom, I knew I would never speak of it to my friends. Wasn't sure what I was afraid of, but I knew it wasn't something I was supposed to see. I've thought about it a lot over the years.

TWENTY-TWO

It was the last weekend of summer vacation. I was anxious about school. Dad was at the embassy, and my mother was visiting a friend at a neighboring apartment building. Tommy went with her because her friend had two little boys around his age. Micheline was in her room. The door was closed. She was listening to music. The French version of "Mammy Blue." I knew the Pop Tops version. It was popular here too. It's a song that always got stuck in your head. I wondered if she was rubbing oil on her legs. That image in my head again. The sudden warm feeling beginning to fill my groin area. I tried to think about something else, but I couldn't shake the image of her legs.

I thought about food.

I went to the kitchen, followed by Buster, and poured myself a bowl of cereal. He sat there and stared. I focused my attention out the sliding-glass balcony door. A large stray cat was chasing a smaller one in the vacant lot until the smaller one jumped onto the cinder-block wall. It was too high for the big one. The smaller cat sat there, as if taunting the other. There was a deep orange-brown sky in the distance, seemed to be coming from the northeast. Didn't look like the kind of sky that would bring a storm, but it was odd—not something I had seen before. The sky did get a comfortable orange at times, but nothing like this. Looked like it was moving our way.

I poured another bowl of cereal, grabbed last weekend's *Washington Post* from the kitchenette, and leafed through until I found the comic strips. I had already read my favorite ones, but I read them again. Finished the cereal, rinsed the spoon and bowl, and set them in the sink.

I walked past her room again but shot the thought of her legs out of my head. Buster jumped on the sofa, turned around a couple of times until he felt the position was right, and plopped down with a groan. I gazed out the sliding-glass door in the living room, toward the south. The sky was clear.

My last weekend of freedom and I was bored to no end. Roddy was out back-to-school shopping with his mom and little sister. I didn't have Lenny's phone number. That was odd. I guess I always depended on Roddy to get in touch with him. Never thought to get it. I walked out to the balcony and around toward my room and the side that faced the playground. Maybe there was some action down there, but it was vacant. Usually a few of the younger kids were out playing. Thought that strange. The thick orange-and-brown sky seemed closer than before. It was like a tremendous cloud that filled the sky. Couldn't even see the mountains. It was weird, even a bit menacing.

The phone in the foyer rang. I ran back to my room and poked my head out the door. Maybe it was Roddy. I heard Micheline answer.

"Yes. Yes. Of course." And then she hung up.

She appeared in the hallway.

"You must help me close all the windows. There is a terrible sandstorm arriving, your father said."

"Sandstorm?"

So that was what it was.

"Cool," I said.

"Close up your bedroom and then check your brother's room, please. I will go to your parents' room."

"Sandstorm. Is it dangerous?"

"Yes, they can be. The winds can be strong, and the sand can fill a room."

I thought about Roddy and wondered if he would get blown away.

"Quickly, now."

I did as she said, closed all the windows up, and went to the living room.

"I will call your mother."

I ran back to my room to look out for the storm. It appeared to be moving fast. Palm trees near the playground were already beginning to sway. The tetherball was being steadily pushed upward. It was a sustaining wind, not gusty. Got heavier by the second.

Someone pounded on the front door. Buster barked, was already at the door by the time I got there. Micheline looked through the peephole, seemed startled.

"Who is this?" she asked.

"Bill Stankey," he said. The voice seemed muffled.

"William?" she said before opening and sounded confused.

"Yes, Ms. Micheline. William Stankey. Is Graham home?"

She opened the door. I sure as hell couldn't tell if that was

Roddy. He was wearing long pants, a long-sleeved shirt, and gloves. He wore his snorkeling mask over his eyes and nose, while the rest of his head and face were covered with a white scarf. He looked like some sort of desert-nomad parody.

Micheline had to hold Buster by the collar.

He stepped in. Micheline couldn't hold Buster. He barked at Roddy.

Roddy took his face mask off and said, "It's me, boy."

Buster wagged his tail and jumped up at him, nearly knocking him over. I pulled him down by the collar.

"Get down, boy," I commanded.

"What are you doing dressed like that?" I asked.

"Going down to ride the wind," he said, his voice muffled by the scarf.

TWENTY-THREE

Buster followed me out to the balcony, but when he felt the heavy wind he turned around and trotted back into my room. The sandstorm was still miles out but looked like it was coming strong. I had never seen anything like it before—an orange-brown, back-sunlit storm cloud. Beautiful and still threatening. I could already feel the fine sand hitting the side of my face, like the beach sand in Acapulco on a windy day, but stronger. I had to squint to prevent the fine grains from getting into my eyes. There were a handful of kids down there, looked mostly like teenagers. Couple of them were wearing ski masks and sunglasses. It didn't look like any of the locals were out. The village looked deserted, the tin and rock structures secured and shut tight. Boards covered the windows. Wooden furniture and crates no longer cluttered the fronts. Anything that could be blown away had been removed, including the backyard chickens. The goats huddled together in their lean-tos, as if they knew what was on the way.

I saw Roddy with someone who looked like Lenny. He was a snowman wrapped in rags and wearing ski goggles. Everyone was goofing off, even spazzy, running around like chickens who see the farmer approaching with their feed.

"Roddy!" I called out, but with no response. "Stankey!" Even louder.

I called out a few more times and then tried Lenny, but still nothing. Drowned out by the wind. I wanted to be down there with them. Then I figured there was no reason I couldn't be. My mother was still visiting the neighbor, getting her early-afternoon drunk in. I didn't think that then, though. It was something I would come to know later in life. Dad had business to attend to at the embassy. Like Mexico, he was gone for much of the time we were there. It was just Micheline, but she forbade me to go out. "Too dangerous," she warned. I always listened to her. But even though she was more of a mother to me than my own mother, she still wasn't my mother. I certainly would not have the occasional thoughts about my mother that I had about Micheline. Oh, even the thought of it. So I walked back into my room, closed and locked the glass door. Buster was sleeping on my bed. I snuck down the hall toward the living room, noticed Micheline's door was closed again. I heard music, but it was lower than before. She'd never know. This was her time off. I could easily sneak out.

I closed my bedroom door behind me and slid open the closet door. I grabbed my swimming mask and leather Chukka boots, set them on the bed, pulled out some long socks from my dresser drawer and some folded-up Levi's from a bottom drawer of the same dresser. I searched for a scarf and head wrap, but didn't find anything. I went to the foyer closet and found what I needed there, including my windbreaker. The scarves belonged to my dad. Went back to my room then and changed up.

I looked in the mirror. Didn't look bad. A bit alienesque, but that was sort of cool. The swimming mask was big enough that it covered my nose. The scarf covered the rest of my face, ears, and neck. I wrapped the tan headscarf as best I could without having a clue how to do it, securing the loose ends under the face mask's straps.

Buster was sleeping on the bed. That's what made him a good apartment dog—he loved to nap. But if I woke him, he'd sense what I was up to and want to go down with me. Do nothing but whine after I left. That'd get Micheline's attention for sure. I quietly stepped out so as not to wake him, closed the door behind me, opened it again to make sure he hadn't woken, then closed it again.

Micheline's door was still shut. French pop music was playing quietly inside. I grabbed my keys next to the phone on the table in the foyer and made a cloak-and-dagger exit.

The elevator opened to howling wind coming up through the shaft. When it opened at the garage area, it was even louder. I could see palm trees bent so low they almost swept the ground. It was definitely a sustained wind, not gusty. Most of the kids were on the paved road on the side of the building, in front of Abu Fouad's store. A couple of older kids from the building were leaning against a car in the open garage. They weren't dressed up like the others. They looked like the Norwegian brothers from the tenth floor.

The wind was coming strong, carrying not only sand but red dirt it had picked up along the way, including from the dirt road where the paved road ended and led up to the hill. Like dirt waves picked up and carried away in a swirl. Despite all that I was wearing, the sand and dirt hitting me below the neck stung—a thousand biting red ants. Especially my hands because damn, I'd forgotten gloves.

I didn't recognize anyone. Their faces were concealed by scarves, sunglasses, and swimming masks. Their arms spread out like wings and bodies literally leaning into the wind so that they were on their toes. It was a loud wind, but I could hear them hollering. Excited, whooping calls. I noticed a couple of kids off on their own. One was Roddy. I recognized the headscarf. His back was to the wind and his arms were stretched out like he was attempting a backstroke. The other kid with him was struggling to walk up the road into the wind.

I stepped out of the open garage area and was almost swept off my feet. I hadn't expected it, but I bent into the wind and walked toward Roddy. He saw me. Yelled something I could not understand. The boy with him turned toward me. It was Lenny.

I looked back to see how far I was from the semi-safety of the open parking garage. Abu Fouad's store was closed. The metal rolling shutters were down.

I slowly made my way to the other boys. Thought I'd be taken off my feet but hunkered into the wind. It was easier to maneuver that way. Lenny stretched his arm out to me. He was wearing leather gloves. I reached out and grabbed his hand with my naked hand, and he helped me over. We all turned to one another and huddled together. A football huddle.

"This something else?" Roddy cried out.

"Yeah," I replied, but wasn't sure about it.

"The wind will actually carry ya," he told me.

"This is crazy, man," I said.

"Yeah," Roddy said. "Watch."

He let go of the huddle and turned to face the wind. Spread his arms out and with a kind of trust I'd never understand, leaned his weight into it. It held him.

"Like flying!" he yelled. "Yee-ha! Riding the wind!"

He was on his toes and got pushed back about two feet down the road. He bent his arms in front, like a blocker preparing to take a hit, then hunched down a bit and walked back toward us.

"It almost took me off my feet," he said.

"Yeah," I replied nervously.

"Just spread your arms and stand on your toes," Roddy advised. "Lean in just a tiny bit."

"Careful you don't get blown to the moon," Lenny teased.

That didn't help, but I had to do it. No way I could back out.

"Watch," Lenny said.

Lenny did it too, but it didn't push him back. He had at least twenty pounds on me and Roddy.

Facing the wind, I spread my arms. My windbreaker was flapping so hard I thought it would be torn off. Despite wearing the swimming mask, I still closed my eyes. I leaned into it, but only a tiny bit, then a bit more. Stood on my toes. Damn if it didn't feel like I *was* flying. I felt myself being moved down the road. Almost weightless. I heard them cheering me on. I opened my eyes. I was slowly sliding down the paved road on my toes. I yelled but didn't know what I was yelling. It felt like time slowed. I was encased in something like a time machine. Then, out of nowhere, something strong grabbed my arm and pulled me out. I turned to face Micheline.

She was wearing a blue, long-sleeved tunic dress. Her

face was wrapped. Her big afro was being blown wild by the wind.

She pulled me to her.

"Come!" she ordered.

I begged her to let me go, that she was embarrassing me. She didn't say a word, just held my arm until we got to the elevator. I could have fought her off, pulled away, but didn't. I thought about how my dad would kick my ass, maybe whip me good.

I noticed Lenny and Roddy watching. I threw my hand up and shot them a fist, like it was all okay. They waved, and gave peace signs with their fingers. Hopefully that meant I had saved face.

On the way up in the elevator, she spoke. Her hair was blown back almost comically, like it had been sculpted into two pointed, blown-back halves.

"I am responsible for you, boy. What if you were carried away into the sea, never to be seen again? What then? What would your parents say?"

How could I answer that? Was that even possible?

"My friends were out there. It was safe."

"I am responsible for you when your parents are not home. Not your friends. You disobeyed."

I knew she didn't have the authority to punish me, but if she told my parents they certainly would.

The elevator door opened on our floor.

"Is my mother home?" I asked nervously.

"No. Thank the Almighty for that."

She unlocked the door and had me go in before her. Buster was barking, not knowing what the hell was standing before him.

"Quiet, boy," I said.

He let out a couple of more yaps. I smacked him on the head and he quieted down.

Micheline took my hand, palm down, and looked it over. Tiny red bumps covered the back of my hands and fingers.

"Oh my," she said. "You come with me to the kitchen. I don't want all this sand to cover the carpet."

I followed her into the kitchen.

"Take all that off," she ordered.

"I'm not taking my pants and shirt off."

"Don't be silly. Just your jacket and covering on your face. That silly-looking mask, too."

I obeyed. Sand from the scarves fell to the vinyl floor. I was worried about my face, if it looked anything like the back of my hands.

"Rinse your hands, but do not dry them off."

I didn't understand, but still did what she asked. She walked out. I noticed her enter her bedroom. She returned a couple of seconds later.

"Sit down, Graham."

I sat. She sat next to me.

"Put your hands out," she said. Her voice calmer now, even comforting.

She poured a bit of oil on her right palm, rubbed it in with both hands. Took my right hand and tenderly rubbed the oil on my hand, paying special attention to the top, where all the red bumps were. The water that I didn't wipe off was absorbed by the oil. She repeated the process on my left hand.

When she finished, she said, "You can take your shoes and socks off."

I did. Fortunately, my feet looked okay. I dumped sand from inside my Chukkas onto the floor.

"And now you give me more work." She smiled after.

"Are you going to tell my parents?" I asked.

"No. Not this time. But only this time," she warned.

She stood up, and went to the sink to wash her hands.

I smelled my hands. They smelled like her.

TWENTY-FOUR

Dad was stationed in Mexico City in 1968, when it hosted the Summer Olympics. My sister was older and more into the games than I was, but it was cool to mingle with the Olympians who walked freely around the stadiums. Mexican soldiers were on hand because of the protests that had taken place before the opening ceremonies. I was young and don't remember much, but during the protest young students had been killed by the soldiers. I later learned they numbered in the hundreds. Regardless of that, my sister and I were allowed to attend both the gymnastics and track events. Our nanny, Raquel, escorted us. I was more interested in the soldiers and the weapons they were carrying than the Olympians.

In September of 1972 Munich hosted the Olympics, and the games brought more death. Tommy and I were only a couple of weeks into the school year when we were taken out because of a curfew. My first curfew. I didn't understand then how something all the way in Munich could possibly endanger us in Beirut.

I was sitting in the den one evening while my dad was smoking a pipe and drinking scotch and reading *The Washington*

Post. It was the second day of the curfew. It was nice not having to go to school, but still there were questions.

"Why do you have to go to work if we have a curfew?"

"Because I have work to do."

"What kind of work?"

"Embassy work."

I shook my head. I'd never get answers.

"Are we in danger here because of what happened?"

"No. They're just being overly cautious."

"But what does Beirut have to do with the Olympians who were murdered?"

"The Israeli Olympians were taken hostage and killed by a group of people that make their home in Lebanon and Syria. Israel borders both countries. We're safe. You don't have to worry."

"I'm not worried."

"That's good."

"I just want to know what's going on."

"These people have been fighting each other for longer than you and I have been alive. I suspect they'll be fighting long after we're gone. When you're old enough to drink scotch, I'll explain."

"I'm old enough."

I remembered the last time, when Dad smeared scotch on my gums. It was awful, but I wanted to know more. I thought maybe it would be different if I drank some. Not as bad.

"Oh, you are?"

"Yes."

"Step on over here, then."

I was reluctant. I thought he was going to goof on me, that he'd never let me drink alcohol. I had always wondered why it was something not permitted, like smoking cigarettes or cigars. Dad opened the door, though. So was I going to find out?

I wanted to.

I walked over, stood to the side of his chair. He offered me the glass. It had several cubes of ice in it and looked like apple juice, so I thought, *How bad could this be?* I took it from him and smelled it, then reeled backward, almost spilling the contents.

"That smells like Buster peed in a fireplace," I said.

He laughed. "You're not old enough."

"I am. I'm almost thirteen."

I brought it to my mouth, plugged my nose with the thumb and index finger of my left hand, and took a tiny sip. Not bad at first, but then I swallowed.

"Ahh! My throat's on fire. It burns," I cried.

Mother walked in, saw me with the glass of scotch in my hand.

"You did *not* just give him alcohol."

"Oh, he barely had a sip. Relax."

"You go rinse your mouth out with water. *Now,*" she ordered.

"It burns," I said again.

"And brush your teeth."

"What were you thinking?" I heard her say as I left.

"It's nothing. Don't get so huffy," he said. "He knows better now."

Not ready? Damn, I didn't think I'd ever be ready for that crap.

TWENTY-FIVE

I could hear them fighting from my room. I closed the door and put the 45 of the English version of "Mammy Blue" on the record player. I played it loud. The constant arguing was starting to get to me. The music helped. Buster was lying on his side at the edge of my bed. I rested my head on his belly, looking toward the ceiling and getting lost in the song.

Oh Mammy. Oh Mammy Mammy Blue, oh Mammy Blue...

We hadn't been told how long the curfew would last. Roddy said he'd been through more than one, and that it didn't change anything: we could still go out and play, hang out at the fort, or even go snorkeling if we wanted. I didn't fully understand. I thought a curfew was something serious, an order you had to obey. According to Roddy, however, it was like a snow day—or rather snow *days*.

My mother opened the door to my room. Didn't even knock like my dad did.

"Turn the music down," she ordered.

That didn't sit right, because I wanted them to turn the *fighting* down—and that was the only reason for the music being played so loud. I did not respond quick enough.

"Did you hear me?" she asked, waving her cigarette like a threat.

"Yes," I said.

"Then turn it down or you'll wake up your brother."

I was slow to respond, but when I did I said, "You probably already woke him up with all your fighting."

"Don't talk to me like that. Now do as I say."

"Go to hell," I blurted out.

She looked stunned. I had never spoken like that before. I knew I had crossed the line. There was no turning back.

She stared. A vacant look. Still no response. She slammed the door.

Dad came in a couple of minutes later. He was holding a tumbler half filled with what looked like scotch.

"What did you just tell your mother?"

What could I say?

"I told her to go to heck."

"I don't think that's quite how you said it. Turn the record player off. Now."

I obeyed.

"You're grounded from listening to it for one week."

"One week? I just repeated what she always says to you. Ground *her*."

"Two weeks. And you will apologize to her first thing in the morning. She'll be calm by then. Go to bed now."

"It's a curfew day. Can't I stay up and read or something?"

"Do you want it to be three?"

"Dang, man."

Grounding me didn't accomplish anything. All it did was make me hate her more.

I tossed and turned my way into sleep, and much later I

woke up to Buster sleeping on my legs. It was constricting and my toes itched because of the lack of circulation. I punched him on the shoulder. He huffed but didn't move. I kicked him out from over me. He stood, circled the edge of the bed a couple of times, and found a comfortable position. In no time he was snoring again.

Still dark out. Took a while to fall back to sleep. When I did, a goliath grouper was there, staring me down. It appeared suddenly from the other side of a sandbar. Scared me awake. That was it for me. Sleep was not my friend that night. I stared through the window until daybreak.

Curfew day. A snow day without snow. At what cost, though? I didn't think about that then. Everything was an adventure. I knew there was death, and I saw the newspaper photographs of the men on balconies wearing stocking caps and bandanas to conceal their identities. It didn't feel real. I had seen so many other images worse than that. Back in the States, when Dad was watching the news and something about Vietnam came on. Back in Mexico City, when the photographs appeared of all those students that the soldiers shot. No, this wasn't like it was real.

It was still too early to get out of bed. I propped myself up on the pillow and thought about what I might do that day. First thing would be to feed and then walk the boy. Buster was my responsibility.

After walking Buster, I returned to the kitchen to grab some breakfast. Micheline was sitting at the table with Tommy. She was reading an English newspaper.

"Those poor young people," she muttered to herself.

I didn't know if she realized I was there. I hung Buster's leash on a hook near the entryway, grabbed a box of cereal, and poured a heaping bowl. The milk was on the table. Tommy was munching away at his cereal.

Micheline folded the paper and set it on the table beside the ashtray. She lit a cigarette, inhaled deep.

"So much hatred," she said.

"Are you mad?" Tommy asked her.

"Not at you, my love. Certainly not you. Eat your breakfast, now."

"Is my dad at work?" I asked.

"Yes, he left early."

"What about her?"

"Her?" She questioned. "You mean your mother?"

"Yeah, I guess."

"You should have respect. She gave birth to you, after all."

I shoved a spoonful of cereal in my mouth.

"Your mother is on the balcony with the early sun, drinking coffee. She is very sad."

"Why?" Tommy asked.

"Because of the massacre," she said.

"What's a massacre?" he asked.

"When many innocents are killed."

"The people that died at the Olympics. They're from Israel," I said.

"Did she know them?" Tommy asked.

"You don't have to know them to be sad about what happened," Micheline said. "Let's not talk about such things anymore. Good thoughts, now."

I wanted to tell her that we had Jewish blood, but remembered what Dad had said. *Micheline wasn't like them, though, was she?* I couldn't imagine she was.

"Mom said you hate her."

"That is not true." Micheline jumped up. "Don't say such things."

"That's what I heard her tell Dad, though."

"There is no hatred in this family."

She looked at me, blew smoke in the air.

"Eat your cereal, Spaz," I told Tommy.

"You boys," Micheline said and picked up the newspaper again, turned to the funnies section, and smiled.

TWENTY-SIX

My mother was sitting on a lounge chair on the balcony, staring off into the horizon. She had on Jackie Onassis sunglasses and wore a black, one-piece bathing suit. Her coffee cup was on the tile floor beside an ashtray. Buster was on his back, legs spread out—a sun dog at heart. She reached over and scratched his chest. For the first time I sort of felt sorry for my mother. *Hate* was just another bad word to me, like cuss words. It usually came from anger. I wasn't so angry anymore. There was still a certain distance between us, though. *Certain* was an understatement. Something I didn't understand then, but would feel inside me for the rest of my life.

I stepped out onto the balcony.

"I'm sorry for cussing at you," I said.

She turned, slid her sunglasses down the bridge of her nose with her index finger—like a movie star.

"I accept your apology. Thank you."

"My friends are all going down to the front to play Kick the Can. Can I go down there?"

"The only reason you apologized was because you needed something. Is that it?"

"No."

Maybe it wasn't the right time to ask for something. Should have waited at least thirty minutes.

"I meant it. I just want to go out and play."

"There's a curfew," she said coldly.

"That's only for the school. It's not a police thing, Dad said."

"It's still a curfew."

"Everyone is out there. Dad said it's safe."

"He did, did he?"

"Yes."

"If I let you go, then Tommy will want to go too. And I don't want him out there, or in here crying to be out there. That wouldn't be fair, would it?"

"It's right out front. We're not going anywhere else. I promise."

"You didn't answer me. What about Tommy? Should I let him cry?"

She was in one of her no-win moods. Didn't matter what I'd say.

"What if I promise to watch Tommy so he can go too?"

She looked at me direct. "There is no way I am letting Tommy go out when there is a curfew."

"Fine, then. I'm grounded from listening to music, and for no reason I can't go outside either. Fine."

I turn to walk away.

"It's not for no reason. There's a curfew."

I turned back to her and said, "So why can the other kids go out?"

"I'm not their parent."

I huffed. I hated her again. But before I could walk away—

"Fine, Graham. Go out there, but be back by dinnertime. And stay in the front."

"I will. Thanks, Mom."

She didn't say anything, just returned to her position in the sun. I left in a hurry before she had a chance to change her mind.

What was the point of all that if she was going to let me go anyway—payback? Hell yeah, that's what I thought. One thing for sure, I didn't feel sorry for her anymore. Maybe I should show her what *bad* really is, like some of those kids back in the States. Fuck bitch shit, yeah, I should.

By the time I got down there most of the kids had scattered. Roddy and Lenny were sitting on the three-foot stone wall that surrounded the playground. Lenny shot me a wave when he saw me.

"What's up?" I said when I got there.

"What's up?" Roddy echoed.

"Thinking about catching lizards in the vacant lot," Lenny said.

"Yeah," I said. "Sounds good to me."

"Think I saw an Agama sunning on a big rock the other day."

"That's a big one," I said. "Mexico had some big ones like that. They were all over the place."

"Here too," Roddy said. "One of the most poisonous snakes in the world lives here."

"*That's* what we should catch," Lenny said.

"Heck yeah," I said. "Gotta get a couple of big sticks to hold it down, though. Those vipers are fat and strong."

"Like Lenny," Roddy laughed.

"All this here is muscle," Lenny returned while pounding his belly with his fists.

That was good for a laugh.

Lenny hopped off the wall, followed by Roddy.

"Let's go," Lenny commanded.

We made our way across the road. Some younger kids, including a couple from the village, were playing Kick the Can. We walked through the garage and a narrow cut that led to the back of the building. Several balconies above had clothing drying on lines.

On the left, toward the road and at the side of the little store, stood Toufique. He was with another larger boy. They were wearing black sweatpants with yellow stripes, and T-shirts with torn sleeves so they looked like tank tops.

It was a long drop over the cinder-block wall to the vacant lot. Too far for us to try. The only way was the little alley off the road and to the side of the building behind ours. That meant we had to walk past Toufique and the other kid.

"Let's go," Lenny said without a thought.

I had never walked that close to Toufique before. He was too much of a threat. Wouldn't do it alone, but with Lenny and Roddy at my side I felt confident. Maybe too confident.

We started walking. Toufique threw some air punches our way. Lenny stopped and jokingly returned some.

"Floats like a bee and stings like a butterfly," he sang. "Butterfly boy." Laughed after.

Toufique stopped throwing punches, turned, and said something to his friend. They both laughed.

"Ha ha," Lenny responded. "Damn spaz."

Roddy laughed. I didn't. I had never been in a fight before, and it felt like this might be my first one. I wasn't ready for that. I wasn't even good at doing push-ups or sit-ups, like most of the other kids my age. I could catch a can or even a fast baseball coming my way, but I'd never had to stop a punch. I couldn't let them know how I felt, and so I simply went along with it. By the time we got close enough to them to pass, Toufique and his Lebanese Lenny stood strong to block our way. We stopped and faced them. The kid with Toufique said something about Americans in Arabic. It didn't sound like a compliment.

Toufique showed off some fancy Ali footwork, his leather sandals skidding back and forth on the sidewalk. Lenny shook his head like it was nothing and started to walk around him. We followed.

"All talk, Americans," Toufique's boy said.

"Muhammad Ali's an American," Roddy said.

"Ali is Muslim," the boy replied, his tone defiant.

"He's American. Just like us. Red-blooded," Lenny challenged.

Out of nowhere, the big boy jumped forward and sucker-punched Lenny in the mouth, knocking him off his feet.

I was stunned. So was Roddy.

Toufique said something in Arabic and threw some unconvincing air punches over Lenny's fallen body. Turned to us, like a dare. Lenny sat up, wiping blood from his lips. He was pissed. And ready. The boy who hit him was long gone.

I don't know what I was thinking, but I belted out a banshee scream and tackled Toufique. He wasn't expecting it. We both fell to the sidewalk, with me on top. I heard a dull *thud* and noticed he was stunned. He seemed surprisingly light, not as big when I was on top of him swinging at his face like I'd lost my mind. And I had. He tried to block my punches with his arms and clenched fists, but all that did was allow me to punch his hands so he was hitting himself. I went crazy on him.

Next thing I knew I was pulled off him like a scrap of paper. I kept punching in his direction, swinging wildly. I was lifted off the ground by whoever was holding me. I noticed he had shiny black combat boots. Military shine, but the pant legs were black. I knew then it was our concierge. He always wore polished combat boots with pressed black pants.

"No more," his voice said from behind me. "*La. La.*"

I stopped struggling and looked up at the concierge.

"Let me go," I demanded. "Let me go!"

"You calm now?"

"Just let me go. He started it."

"I let you go. No more. Right?"

"Yes," I said, winded.

He let me go.

Lenny was standing up and ready to pounce on Toufique, who lay on his back with a swollen left eye.

"*La!*" the concierge ordered.

Roddy was on the other side of Lenny. He had his fists up.

Abu Fouad was out of the store and looking at us sternly. He yelled something at Toufique, who pushed himself off the ground, wiped the blood from his mouth with the back of his hand, and looked at me with murder in his eyes. Abu Fouad shouted out another order in Arabic. Toufique was reluctant, still ready to fight me, but he turned and walked with a huff into the store.

TWENTY-SEVEN

Micheline said my mother had gone to the Phoenician Hotel with Roddy's mom. I knew that meant the bar. We were all sitting around the dinette table in the kitchen. Except Tommy. He was standing and hovering over Lenny, looking at the blood trickling from his lip. Buster was sitting near Lenny's chair, thinking he was being fed something and he'd vacuum up whatever dropped to the floor. There were poker cards on the table. Micheline had been playing some card game with Tommy when we came in.

"Does it hurt?" Tommy asked.

"Naw," Lenny said.

Micheline was tending to Lenny's split lip with ice wrapped in a towel.

A couple of knuckles on my right hand had bandages on them. I had washed my hands and taken care of those myself. I wasn't so hyped anymore.

"You are not my responsibility, boy, and here I am taking care of you too."

"Thank you, ma'am."

"What will your mother think?" she asked.

"It wasn't his fault," I said. "He was attacked."

"And this boy—Toufique's friend. You said you don't know him?"

"No. The concierge said he would take care of it," Roddy said.

"Yeah, the concierge was sitting on the other side of the store. Was right there," Lenny added.

"You will tell your mother, boy."

"Yes, ma'am," Lenny said.

"And your father will take care of this nonsense when he comes home," she told me.

"It wasn't our fault," I said.

"You have said that already."

After she stopped the bleeding from Lenny's lip, she went to the refrigerator and grabbed three bottles of orange soda. Handed each of us one.

"Me too," Tommy said.

"No more sugar for you. You have too much sweet in you already."

"We're going to go to my room," I told her.

"Yes. No more downstairs for the day."

"Buster, c'mon, boy," Roddy said.

Buster happily obeyed and we walked out.

In my room I asked Roddy to shut the door.

Lenny looked through the records on my dresser.

"I can't play any music now," I said.

"What do you mean?"

"My dad grounded me from using the record player."

"Dang, how long?" Roddy asked.

"The rest of this week."

"What'd you do?"

"Told my mom to go to hell," I said.

"Damn, you beat the crap outta the Butterfly Boy and told your mom to go to hell. Going to start calling you G-Man from now on," Lenny said.

The nickname stuck.

Dad didn't come home for dinner that night. My mother said he got stuck at work. Before bed I did twenty push-ups and thirty sit-ups. I took off my T-shirt and flexed my muscles in front of the dresser mirror. Looked good, especially with the Band-Aids on my knuckles. My first fight, and I'd won. Sort of.

The next morning I ate breakfast at the dinette table with Dad and Tommy. My mother was still in bed. Dad said she wasn't feeling well, so we should keep it down inside. We ate scrambled eggs with toast, butter, and blueberry jam. Tommy and I had a bowl of cereal on the side. Micheline was out on the kitchen balcony, hanging clothes on the line to dry. Dad put the newspaper down after reading only the front page.

"Tell me about the fight," he said.

"Graham beat a Lebanese boy up," Tommy jumped in.

"Shut up," I said.

"Watch that," Dad warned.

"We didn't start it," I explained. "We were looking around the building trying to find lizards when Toufique and this other kid we didn't know blocked us from walking. We tried to walk around and the other kid pounced on Lenny, hit him in the face and knocked him to the ground."

"For no reason?"

I hesitated. Always a mistake. "Yeah."

"You guys didn't say anything to egg them on, maybe provoke them?"

"Not that I know."

He knew better.

"Okay, the kid who hit Lenny told him Muhammad Ali wasn't an American, and Lenny told him he was."

"And that's why the other boy punched Lenny?"

"Yes. That's the truth."

He looked at me but not hard—not like he was about to interrogate me and break me down.

"Okay, I'll have a talk with Toufique's father and Abu Fouad."

"No, Dad. Please. That'll just make it worse, 'cause—"

"*Because*," he corrected me.

"Because he'll get in trouble and blame it on us."

"Then you promise me this: next time you see them, you walk the other way. There's no shame in that. We're the visitors here."

"And that means they can do what they want? Beat us up when they want?"

"Absolutely not. They come for you, you defend yourselves. Otherwise, you keep out of their way."

"Okay."

"I have to go to work." He drank the rest of his pressed coffee, set it down, and got to his feet. "Remember, boys, let your mom sleep in, okay? Micheline is in charge."

"All right," I said.

He rubbed the top of Tommy's head and gave the back of mine a light slap before exiting.

"You got in trouble," Tommy teased.

"I did not. He would have whipped me if I got in trouble. Eat your cereal or I'll whip you."

"I'll tell."

"You're a rat fink."

TWENTY-EIGHT

A little over a week later, the curfew was extended—this time by the Lebanese government. Roddy and I were outside at the time despite orders to stay in. I told my mother I was going to Roddy's apartment and he told his mom he was going to mine. We heard the sky roar, looked up and saw two jets flying low, headed south. Before they were out of our sight we heard the explosions, but they seemed farther away than where the jets were. We ran inside, but not to our apartments. We went to the roof.

Blooms of smoke, like pencil-drawn mushrooms in the distant sky, appeared one after the other. Explosions quickly followed. It sounded like short bursts of thunder a couple of seconds after lightning appeared. We could see the jets. They were far away, small enough to pinch between our thumbs and index fingers.

"Those bombs look like they're going off in the area where we were camping," Roddy said.

"You think?" I questioned.

"Damn. Are we at war?"

"*We?* This isn't our country. Why would we be at war?"

"Yeah, you're right. Maybe Israel."

"Yeah. Maybe."

"My dad said we can't go near the windows, and we're sleeping on the floor beside our beds."

"Yeah, us too. That's common stuff."

"I don't mind it, though," I said.

"Naw, me either. I made a tent with my blankets. Pretty cool."

"I gotta do that too."

"Yeah," Roddy said.

We sat at the edge of the building behind a short wall that surrounded the roof. Every time a bomb exploded, we'd say something like *wow* or *dang*, like it was the Fourth of July.

TWENTY-NINE

The night after the bombings Dad had a man from the embassy over for dinner. He was an odd man, with a quirky half smile and a squinty left eye, like the muscles on the left side of his face had stopped working. He had a nickel-sized dent in his left cheek. Looked like a bullet hole that healed up. Dad later told me that it was. He was shot while on a tour in Vietnam. Swallowed most of his teeth but spit the bullet out and continued to fight. "He has to wear dentures," Dad said, like it was funny. His name was James Hawthorne.

After dinner they retired to the den with my mother for drinks. Tommy and I were allowed to stay in the living room. I thought I'd be a good brother and play with him and his GI Joes.

"Stay away from the windows," Dad said.

"That'd be a good idea," said the man with a hole in his cheek.

I sat against a wooden chair with cushions. I took the back cushion off and set it on the end of the chair to lean against and to conceal my head from their view in the den. It was near the large archway that led into the den, so I could hear them well. Buster sat in front of me, with Tommy on the other side.

"Buster's the hill," I told Tommy.

"Good. I can blow him up."

"No, this hill can't be blown up. You're the enemy and I have to take the hill from you."

"Why do I have to be the enemy?"

"Because I'm GI Joe, that's why."

"I'm GI Joe. See?" He showed me the second GI Joe he had in his collection.

"There can only be one GI Joe and that's me. You want me to play or not?"

"All right," he said with a bit of reluctance.

I could hear them talking in the den, mostly about good restaurants to check out or nightspots where Mr. Hawthorne said my dad should take my mother. Polite conversation. Boring.

I wasn't paying attention and Tommy managed to get most of his soldiers over the hill of Buster. I quickly knocked them down. One of them hit Buster near his nose. He sniffed it, then licked it up and into his mouth.

"Buster, no!" Tommy said, trying to open Buster's mouth to retrieve the soldier.

Buster spit it out, having realized it wasn't food. It was chewed up, with part of one leg broken off.

"Bad Buster," Tommy said.

Tommy picked it up.

"He's dead," I told him. "A land mine. In fact, all your men are dead. It was a big explosion."

"No fair. I got over Buster."

"His mouth is a land mine. Killed all your men. I win."

"You cheated. Knocked all my soldiers over. He wouldn't have hit the land mine if you didn't do that."

"Well, life isn't fair, is it? Learn to live with it."

"We're just playing a game."

"Same thing, so shut up."

"Quiet in there," my mother said.

"War is hell," I heard the man say.

The game was over. I sat where I was to continue spying on the conversation. Tommy picked up all his pieces and went to the other side of the living room to play on his own. Buster stayed where he was. I rested my feet over him.

My mother excused herself after a few minutes, came into the living room, and sat on the couch to read a magazine and smoke cigarettes. I rested my head back on the cushion, trying to be as covert as possible so my mother wouldn't know I was eavesdropping. The man, John Hawthorne, interested me a great deal, and I wanted to know what they were talking about. A man who swallowed his teeth and spit out a bullet had to say something worth hearing. I looked at my mother. She had stubbed out the cigarette in an ashtray on the coffee table and was nursing another martini.

I listened in.

"They hit strategic targets, but I don't think they're done," Mr. Hawthorne said.

"Agreed," Dad said. "The Israelis won't stop there."

"Some of the locals I'm working with said the PLO was prepared. Casualties were minimal, and we're talking what, a couple of tanks and bridges?"

"You can't always trust the locals that work for you. I learned that much in Cuba."

"I take most of what intelligence they give me with a grain of salt."

"What do you think of the scotch?"

"Damn fine," Mr. Hawthorne said. "I know you can't get it here."

"No, you can't. I brought a case in from the States. One of the bottles has your name on it if you want it."

"I damn well won't turn that down." He looked toward my mom with a quirky half smile. "Seems you have all the fine stuff."

I was too young to understand what he meant.

Dad didn't have time to respond.

"It's time for you kids to go to bed," my mother said.

"C'mon, Mom—there's no school tomorrow."

"Yeah," Tommy agreed.

"Listen to your mother," Dad said from the other room.

"I don't want to sleep on the floor alone," Tommy whined.

"I'm going to read in bed, sweety, so I'll be right there with you."

"Can I stay up just twenty more minutes?" I asked.

"No." My mother was firm.

Dad had bought me a new sleeping bag after the other one was taken by the river when we went camping. The new one was a better bag with more padding. I had it on the floor to the side of the bed that didn't face the window and the sliding-glass door. There was a makeshift tent over the sleeping area. I used one of Dad's bedsheets because it was bigger, securing it on the edge of the bed at one end with pillows and at the other end on the floor with several of my books. The curtains in my room were drawn. Buster jumped on the bed first thing, started twirling to find a sleep position.

"Down, boy," I said. "You're sleeping in the tent with me."

He didn't obey, just plopped down with his big body in a fetal position.

"I said *down,* Buster."

I grabbed him by the collar and had to drag him off the bed. His front end dropped to the floor, but his rear end and legs stayed up. He didn't move. I pulled at him. He finally gave in, stretched his hind legs so they'd slide on the bed and off to hit the floor. I went into the tent to get myself comfortable first, then called for Buster.

"Careful, boy. Don't knock down the tent."

He walked to the back of the tent and lay at my feet, then turned so his head was facing the exit. Despite the lack of room, he found a comfortable position.

"Good boy."

I had my flashlight by the pillow. I scooted out and took the cord for the lamp on the nightstand. Pulled the plug out of the socket to turn the light off.

I heard shooting that night. In the distance. Little pops. One after the other. There was only one explosion, though.

THIRTY

The bombings stopped after about three days. There was still a curfew, but from the living room balcony I noticed the Pigeon Man exercising his pigeons and a couple of fishermen on the reefs. A few people were walking along the promenade, and the traffic along the Corniche was steady. I'd have to go back to school soon.

Roddy was skittish that afternoon in Chameleon Fort. I was sure it had to do with everything from having to sneak out during a curfew and the bombings to the skirmish we'd had with Toufique and his buddy. A lot to worry about. I was worried too, but the apprehension added to the adventure. We weren't supposed to be there. Our parents forbade us from leaving the building, yet there we were. If Toufique and company discovered this spot, it'd be over. A lot could go wrong. Things we didn't worry about before. A bomb could drop on us for all we knew. Maybe one would.

There wasn't much to surveil. Tenants were staying clear of their balconies. Even the Druze village seemed lifeless, like everyone had moved. Just stupid boys like us dared to venture out. We did notice two tanks headed south. We looked at each other like maybe we should leave. The adventure seemed like it was turning south with the tanks. Maybe more bombings.

"What's that?" Roddy whispered.

"What?"

"Shh. Listen."

I heard rustling, like someone or something moving toward us.

"Keep still," I whispered.

It was closer.

It stopped. We jumped off our butts when a small stone broke through the top of the thicket, nearly hitting me on the head. Another one was tossed right after that. Then another. And another. Damn. We looked at one another and Roddy mouthed *Toufique*. We were blown. The fort we had sweated and bled over was done. We'd have to fight our way out. But the rocks weren't being thrown with force. They just seemed to drop over us like they were being lobbed.

I picked up my binoculars. We were both ready to make a break for it when Lenny popped through the opening.

"Hello in there," he said with a big grin.

Roddy punched him on the shoulder.

"You scared the piss outta us, man," I said. "Get in before someone sees you."

He crawled in. Had a small knapsack with him.

"Brought refreshments," he said.

He opened it, and to our great surprise pulled out a bottle of A&W Root Beer.

"I have one bottle left."

"You were holding out on us," Roddy said.

"You brought that back from the States?" I asked.

"Yep."

He popped it open, took a swig, passed it over to me and I did the same, then passed it over to Roddy. We took our time drinking and savoring it.

"You see the big tanks on the Corniche?" Lenny asked.

"Yeah," I said.

"They're gearing up. Looks like more trouble," Lenny said.

"Maybe we should go in," I said.

"Naw," said Lenny. "Don't be a wuss."

"I'm not a wuss."

"Thought you couldn't get out?" Roddy asked like he was changing the subject.

"My mom went to a neighbor's house and I told her I was going to your place."

"Nice," Roddy said.

"Can't stay, though. Have to get back before my mom, or that'll be the end of me."

"Aww, man . . ." Roddy said.

"War is hell," I said.

PART TWO

THIRTY-ONE

He was dead for sure. It had been only a couple of minutes but felt like an hour. Roddy had left shortly after Lenny did. I was alone. The fallen man's eyes remained open. Had a soft, milky-eyed stare. It was that fast. Never seen anything like it before. The other man was still there, standing over the body. I wondered if he needed to make sure. I was terrified. I swear I could hear my heart beating, echoing out through the fort. If the man bent down to inspect the dead man more thoroughly, he'd easily see me through the open areas between the thickets' branches.

My chest was heaving as I tried to catch my breath. I couldn't move. Too damn scared to do anything. How long was this man going to stand there, and what if someone else walked by? In fact, what if he was waiting for someone else? I looked toward the opening. It was about two yards from the body, maybe less from where the man was standing. I thought about making a break for it. *No, safer to stay here—wait it out.* I shook my head as if trying to convince myself.

I heard the man shuffling his feet through the brush but couldn't tell if he was leaving. I peeked through an open portion of the branches. His arms were reaching down toward the dead man's legs. I saw him clench the ankles but couldn't make out the killer's face.

"Damn fool," he said angrily.

He was an American.

The body was moved a few inches. I saw the head sliding along the dirt. It startled me. I breathed in a gulp of air. The man had let go of the legs.

He called out something in broken Arabic, like a question. I didn't know if it was to someone else or if he had heard me. I heard him move. Closer. The machete blade stabbed through the roof of our thicket. Not close enough to hit me, though. Next time, maybe.

He said the same thing again, and I think he swung the machete over the branches at the top, but it didn't break through. Dead leaves fell all around me. Probably a spider or two. That's when I made the decision to run. I slowly scooted toward the opening. The man wasn't that far away, but he also wasn't so close that I didn't want to chance it. I had to get out. I was sure that he would find the opening. If that happened, I would have no place to run. I'd be trapped in the thicket.

I got myself as close to the opening as I could without poking my head out. I surveyed the area to the left. Could not see him. He was on the other side of the thicket. I broke out, got to my feet, and ran. I was running so fast I thought I'd lose my feet from under me.

I didn't know if the man was running after me, but I didn't want to look back and take the chance he'd see my face. I tore past the kids playing on the playground.

I dashed down the paved portion of the road to the

sidewalk, where I almost had to skid to a stop to avoid crashing through the front glass door of Abu Fouad's store.

I opened the door and ran in.

"Call the police!" I shouted. "*Policia!*" I shouted again, but in Spanish because I wasn't thinking straight.

Abu Fouad stood there behind the counter, looking at me like I'd gone mad.

Abu Fouad spoke in a harsh tone—something in Arabic—and waved his hands to shoo me out of the store. Last person he wanted to see was me. I ignored him, tried to make him understand that I needed the police. He didn't understand.

I peered out the front store window, toward the direction I ran from.

I turned back to Abu Fouad.

"Concierge?" I pled with Abu Fouad and then began to cry.

He moved from behind the counter and literally pushed me out the store like I was a goat.

"Yella," he said.

The only word I understood. I obeyed and hurried out of the store but stood near the front door.

I ran around the back and through the cut that led to the elevator and the stairs. I ran up the stairs to the fourth floor, where Roddy lived. I pounded on his door.

He answered.

I couldn't catch my breath.

"What's going on?" he asked. "Why's your face wet?"

"Who is it, sweetie?" I heard his mom ask.

"It's Graham, Mom. Just Graham."

"We need to talk," I said. "In your room."

"What's going on?"

"Now," I demanded.

Roddy's apartment was the same model as ours. He didn't have someone like Micheline to take care of them and the house, so the little bedroom had been made into an office for his mom and dad. His dad was an English teacher at the American Community School. They had lived there for a while.

Roddy's bedroom was down the hall next to the bathroom like my bedroom. His bed and his dresser were in the same place as mine too, but he had built-in shelves that held books, records, stacks of comic books, and action figures. He had a nice stereo system on a center shelf. Much nicer than mine. Posters on the wall, too: The Hulk, Spiderman, Aquaman, a big map of Lebanon. Framed family photographs hung above the dresser.

First thing I did was go to the sliding-glass door and pull back the curtain a little to look out.

"What the heck is going on?"

"Can't see anyone over there."

"Did you get in another fight with Toufique?"

"No—but I think I saw someone get killed."

THIRTY-TWO

O h, shit. I left my binoculars at the fort." I remembered after telling Roddy what happened.

"Damn, don't tell me they have your name etched on them."

"Just my dad's initials."

"Damn, damn, damn."

He plopped his butt down on the edge of the bed.

"No way out of this. We have to tell our parents," he said.

"I'll be grounded for life."

"It's the right thing, though, isn't it?"

"I guess."

"And I know a lot of the kids, especially the boarders, go out during curfews. It's not like you're breaking the law or anything."

"I guess you're right. I mean, it's not like something I can keep to myself. Is it?"

"Hell no. That might even be a crime. I read in one of my detective comics that a man got arrested for keeping information from the police."

"That's America, though."

"Gotta be the same here."

"Or worse."

Roddy and I thought that withholding information about a murder would have had more serious repercussions than disobeying my parents and breaking curfew. That's what we thought at the time. It changed quickly. My dad was a punisher, and more than likely this would involve the most serious punishment I had ever experienced. That's what I thought at the time. A few belts to the ass'd be nothing. That's why we decided there was more strength in sticking together and getting Lenny in on it. Withhold the information for now.

Roddy called Lenny from a phone in his foyer, told him it was of the utmost importance that he come over.

"Right away. Not messing around. I can't say over the phone. Okay. Okay. See you in a minute."

"He said his mom is back so he can come down."

"Good."

Roddy kept an eye through the peephole until he saw Lenny step out of the elevator.

He opened the door and let him in.

"What's up?" Lenny asked, sounding winded.

His lip was still a little swollen from the sucker punch, and now his left eye was puffy and purplish black in color. He didn't have that before.

"What happened to your eye?" Roddy asked.

"Oh, nothing. My dad came home early, was trying to teach me how to block a sucker punch is all."

"Didn't think you could block a sucker punch," I said.

"Looks that way, doesn't it?"

"Let's go to my room," Roddy said, trying to get back on topic.

Back in the room, Roddy grabbed his desk chair, slid it over toward the side of the bed. He walked back and closed the door.

"You might want to sit down," he said.

"C'mon, what's going on?"

"Just sit down, Lenny," Roddy said.

Lenny sat. Both Roddy and I sat at the edge of the bed facing him.

"G-Man has something to tell you," Roddy said in a serious tone.

"What? What? You guys are killing me."

"About half an hour after Roddy left the fort, I saw a man get murdered," I blurted out.

"What? Is this some kinda joke, you two?"

"No," I said.

"Is that all you're going to say?" Roddy asked. "Tell him everything."

"Okay," I said, "give me a second."

"You're kidding, right?" Lenny pursued.

"Here's the story," I began again.

I told him everything. Didn't spare a single detail, including the blood I saw seeping from the dead man's lip. And that he looked familiar. I had seen him somewhere before and was pretty sure it was when Roddy and I were getting shawarmas uptown.

"You never told me that," Roddy said.

"I just remembered."

"If this is a joke, you guys are doing a good job, I'll tell ya."

"It's not a joke," I said. "I really saw it."

"Did you tell your dad?"

"No. Not yet."

"Then you have to tell him. I mean now."

"I'm going to get my hide tanned for breaking curfew," I said, having second thoughts.

"I think that's the last thing you have to worry about. What if the murderer saw you when you ran?"

"I didn't look back, and he was farther back from the opening."

"Still. You don't know."

Lenny stood up and walked to the window, opened the curtain a bit, and peeked through.

"Can you see where the man was from up here?"

We both walked over, opened the curtain a little more so we could all look out.

"Not really," I said. "But it was on the other side of the fort there. The part that's blocked by the wall."

"And you left your binoculars there?"

"Yeah."

"Damn, man. What about the root beer bottle? Did you leave that?"

"Of course. Who'd think about grabbing that after witnessing someone getting murdered?"

"Well double damn, man. If the murderer searched the fort, then he found the root beer bottle and he'll know you're American. No one else but Americans would be drinking root beer—especially A&W."

"Crap," I said.

"Yeah, crap. And it's a well-known fact in the American community here that I drink a lot of root beer," Lenny said.

"How could the murderer ever know that?" Roddy asked.

"You tell me?" Lenny said seriously.

We thought about it for a second or two but couldn't come up with anything.

"We brought you here because I need your advice," I said.

"It seems to me that we need to see if the body is still there first," Lenny said.

"Are you crazy?" I said. "The killer might be there."

"Then he's a stupid killer, because how does he know you didn't already call the police?"

"Because they'd be down there by now."

"Or staking it out," Lenny said. "See if the killer returns to the body."

"Why would he do that?" I asked.

"Good question," said Roddy.

"Maybe he didn't have time to dispose of the body because of you. Maybe he left a clue on the man he murdered. I don't know."

"That's really doubtful," Roddy said. "I mean that he'd return to the body."

"I've read that killers like to return to the scene of the crime," I said. "Then he could still be staking it out."

"Yes, that's true," Lenny said.

"Agreed," Roddy said.

"So what the hell do we do?" I asked.

"Well, we could walk your dog close to the area," Lenny began. "See if we see the body. It'll be three of us with a dog and not two."

"Too risky," I said. "Maybe I should just tell my dad."

"What if the man is still alive? Then you don't have to say anything, just get someone to help him."

"Who?"

"Abu Fouad."

"I tried that. He kicked me out of his store. Didn't under-stand a word I was saying."

"Then the concierge or someone from the village."

"Lenny might be right. I say we all walk down to the area with my dog, act all normal. Do that first. He's probably not even there anymore," I said.

"You guys are nuts."

"You have to show us the body," Lenny said. "I need to see it."

"I say we wait until tomorrow," I said.

"Why don't we just stake it out from here for a while, see what happens?" Roddy suggested.

"I like that idea."

"I need to see the body," Lenny persisted. "There's three of us, and your monster dog. We have strength in numbers."

"I agree with Roddy. Let's watch from here first."

"Okay, then. We'll do it your way," Lenny said.

"And I think we should go tomorrow. Give it a day. We can still watch from here, though," I said. "I mean, I really don't want to go down there yet."

"If there's a dead man, we should go today."

"If he's dead he'll be there tomorrow," I said.

"Or not," Lenny said.

"But it doesn't really matter, right?" Roddy asked. "I mean, because you saw what you saw."

"I did."

"Okay then. Tomorrow. First thing," Lenny relented. "We'll do it your way."

THIRTY-THREE

Good thing about the curfew was we were the only Americans in our neighborhood out and about—or rather the only ones stupid enough to sneak out. It was about 10 a.m. Buster was excited to be out. My dad usually walked him in the morning, but I could use the excuse that he was whining to go out so I'd had to take him. He pulled me toward the cinder-block wall, an area he had designated by urination to be his. Lenny and Roddy followed. We were vigilant, keeping our eyes on the hill area. The Pigeon Man wasn't out. I wondered if that meant something, because he usually was.

After Buster did his business and sniffed around his territory, we slowly made our way toward the hill.

I stopped after only a few steps.

"Guys. We shouldn't be doing this. I got a bad feeling."

"I have to see the body," Lenny said. "If it's still there, I mean."

"You just want to see a dead body," Roddy told him. "That's perverse."

"I'm not a pervert."

"Then why do you want to risk going up there to see a dead body? What if the murderer is waiting?" I asked.

"Why would he be waiting? Unless he's stupid."

"Maybe he *is* stupid!"

"Let's just get this over with and get out of here," Roddy said.

Buster caught a good scent, stopped to take it in. I jerked the leash, tightening the choke chain. He grunted, trying to use his weight to stay. I jerked again.

"C'mon, you mutt. Smell for bad guys."

After a couple more sniffs he followed.

We stayed close to the wall.

"Watch for snakes," Lenny warned.

"Buster'll do that," I said, but I knew he wouldn't. He'd sniff it, probably get his nose bit, and that'd be another problem we'd have to deal with.

Lenny patted him on his big head, said, "Good boy."

Buster wagged his tail a few times, sniffed the area in front of him like it was his job. He stopped in his tracks, smelled something in the air. He made a whining sound. Sniffed some more.

"You think he smells the body?" Lenny asked.

"I don't know. He usually acts like that when he smells another dog. C'mon, boy."

I jerked his chain again. He seemed reluctant, but obeyed.

"Be sure to look out for flying rocks," Roddy said.

"I think Toufique is banned from the area. Haven't seen him since the fight," I reassured him.

"Doubt that," Roddy said. "His dad owns the building. He can do what he wants. Just keep an eye out."

"Let's just get to the body, if it's still there, and get the hell out of here," I said.

"Hell yeah. Sounds good to me."

I was afraid, but also excited. I didn't know why at the time. It was a dead body, after all. It was the same feeling I had when I was a rookie cop going to my first death scene. It was not so much the fear that came with danger, but how your body would react when you saw something that shouldn't be seen. Would I vomit? Freeze? Both?

When I'd first seen the man on the ground, I hadn't had time to think about such things. When danger kicked in, I ran. I looked at Roddy and could tell he was feeling something similar. Scared, but excited. I don't think Lenny had enough sense to feel scared. He just wanted to see a corpse.

We stopped where the wall ended below the hill.

"It should be around the corner of the wall," I whispered. "I'll stay here with Buster and be the lookout."

"Hell no. Buster'll be the first one to alert us if someone's there," Lenny said quietly.

Buster sniffed the air. Whimpered quietly, like he was excited.

"He definitely smells something," I said.

"Let's go, then," Lenny said.

"You're the one who wanted to see if the body was here," I countered.

"Yeah, but we go as a team. You came to me, remember?"

"I'll go," Roddy said bravely.

He surveyed the area and snuck around the corner.

We let him go, but Lenny followed soon after. I didn't like being alone, so I joined them.

The opening of the fort was still intact.

The man was still where he fell, but covered with brush. His feet were sticking out a bit. Flies were gathered on the ground and around his stomach area, where the blood had dried to a dark purplish color. Buster tried to pull me there, excited by the smell.

"Damn. There he is," I said.

"Oh wow, are you sure he's dead?" Lenny asked.

"I'm not going to check," I said.

Lenny searched the ground, found a large stick.

He scooted around, staying close to the wall of the fort, but getting close to the feet.

He poked the feet with the stick.

Flies swarmed out from the brush. We swatted at them.

"Maybe he's just unconscious," Roddy said.

Lenny moved closer.

Buster pulled me over. I tried to stop him. He got close to the man's feet and sniffed. I yanked him hard and wrapped the leash around my wrist to tighten it up. I saw a bit of the man's face under the dried-up brush. His eyes looked to be still open. Flies were on him. On his eyes. I turned, dragged Buster down toward the wall, and puked.

Buster tried to smell my vomit. I had to yank him hard again. Roddy saw my vomit and then he heaved too.

"You guys gonna be okay?" Lenny asked.

I nodded, took the bottom of my T-shirt and wiped my mouth.

Lenny used the stick to remove the brush from his face. More flies flew out. Swarmed around the body.

"His eyes are still open," Lenny said. "I've never seen any-thing like it. Oh man."

"Okay. Okay. We've seen what we need to see, now let's go. Please," I said.

"He doesn't look real," Roddy said. "Poke him to make sure."

"Let's go. This isn't right," I said.

Lenny poked through the brush, tapping at the man's stomach.

"He's dead for sure," Lenny said.

"We should leave this to the authorities," I advised. "Don't mess up the crime scene."

I went to the opening of the fort, let Buster poke his head in first. I bent down and crawled ahead of him.

"My damn binoculars are gone!" I said.

"My root-beer bottle—is it there?"

"No one cares about the damn root-beer bottle, Lenny," Roddy said.

"I do. It can be tied to me."

"How the hell can it be tied to you?"

"I told you, everyone knows I bring back a lot of root beer from the States. I'm the guy you go to."

"I would say that is highly unlikely," I said.

I stood up, faced them. "A man's dead. Let's get the hell outta here. Now."

Before leaving, Lenny crawled partway into the fort and grabbed his bottle.

"You and your damn root beer," Roddy said.

I turned and began walking toward the road. They quickly followed.

THIRTY-FOUR

We went to my apartment. My mother was in the living room with Tommy, reading a magazine. Didn't even bother to look up at us when we entered. Tommy was playing with his Tonka trucks. Buster was panting. I pulled his collar off and he trotted into the kitchen. Micheline poked her head out, cigarette in her mouth.

"We're going in my room," I told her.

She inhaled the cigarette, took it out of her mouth between two fingers and said, "Keep noise down. Will your friends be staying for lunch? I will make grilled cheese."

"Heck yeah," Lenny said.

"No, thank you," I said.

"Aww, man!"

"Think about what we just saw," I whispered. "How can you think about eating?"

Buster strolled out of the kitchen and into the living room, plopped on the carpet near the sofa. Tommy pushed one of the Tonka trucks over to him, rolled it over his back like he was a hill.

I closed the door to my room, went to the record player,

turned it on, and set the needle on the record. Side One of Jethro Tull's *Thick as a Brick* started. I turned the volume down a bit.

"What's wrong with your mom?" Roddy asked. "She never talks."

"She hates it here," I said.

I was sure she hated me too but didn't mention that.

"What's to hate?" Lenny asked.

"I guess she hates everything."

"This is a good record," Roddy said. "I still have to turn you onto America."

"I like America," Lenny said.

"You guys are something else. What are we going to do?"

"You have to tell your dad," Roddy said.

"How do I explain all this?"

"You had to walk Buster. You saw the body."

"Yeah. I didn't want him to do his business in the apartment."

"That works," Lenny said.

"I'll call my dad. Can you guys stay here with me in case I need some backup?"

"Yeah."

"Yeah, man."

I turned the record player off.

"Wait here."

I walked to the foyer. My mother was still reading.

"I have to call Dad about something," I told her.

"That's fine," is all she said.

I picked up the phone. The line was long enough so that I could take it to the hallway. I dialed his number.

"Mr. Sanderson, please," I said when his secretary answered. "His son."

I told him the lie about having to walk Buster. Surprisingly, he wasn't that angry. Then I told him about the body. There was an uncomfortable pause.

"What do you mean *a body*?"

I explained.

"Probably just an unconscious drunk. You should not have been wandering around the hill during curfew. Next time, stay close to the building."

"He's dead, Dad. Roddy—Bill and Lenny were with me. He's dead for sure."

"Who is Roddy?"

"That's Bill's nickname."

"I'll come home for lunch. You stay put," he said firmly.

I hung up, placed the phone back on its cradle, and walked back to my room.

"He's gonna tan my hide," I told them.

"He said that?" Roddy asked.

"Just sounded like it. He's coming home for lunch. You guys can wait, right?"

"I should call my mom," Lenny said.

"Me too."

"Strength in numbers, remember?" I said.

About forty-five minutes later Dad came home. I was thankful Lenny and Roddy were there. He wouldn't tan my hide with them around. They'd buy me some time.

We were listening to Jethro Tull's *Aqualung* when Dad walked in the room. Based on the look he had, he hadn't expected my friends to be there. He was wearing a navy-blue seersucker suit with a dark blue tie. He usually dressed down—khakis and a short-sleeved guayabera shirt from Mexico City.

"Boys," he said like a hello.

"Sir," Lenny said.

"Hello, Mr. Sanderson."

"So what is it you got yourselves into?"

"Nothing, Dad. I swear. I had to take Buster out because he was whining. They went with me."

"Yes sir," Lenny confirmed.

"Buster smelled something and pulled me to where the dead man was."

"Again, what makes you think he's dead and not some fallen drunk?"

"All the blood," I said.

THIRTY-FIVE

Dad had us go to the balcony and point out the area.

"Right around the corner of the big wall where that twisted old tree is," I said. "There's a large thicket, and he's on the ground to the right."

"Did you tell your mother about this?"

"No," I said. "Just told you. I tried to tell Abu Fouad, but he didn't understand me."

"I'll go see. You boys wait for me here."

"But we can show you exactly where it is," I said.

"No. You're going to wait here," he ordered.

Roddy and Lenny didn't say anything, but I could tell by their expressions they were equally disappointed.

Dad walked out of the room. We waited on the balcony for him until he appeared stepping out from the garage area.

He made his way up the road. I noticed Abu Fouad standing on the sidewalk at the corner of the building. He was watching Dad as he approached the hill.

"Old Abu Fouad," I said. "He wouldn't even help me."

"I'm not allowed to go in there," Roddy said. "He doesn't have anything worth buying anyway."

We couldn't see my dad when he walked around the corner of the tall wall. Abu Fouad stepped back under the building in the direction of his store. Shortly thereafter, Dad appeared. He looked up at us on the balcony but didn't acknowledge us.

He disappeared under the building. I ran to the foyer, followed by Roddy and Lenny.

"What are you three up to?" my mother asked.

"Just waiting for Dad."

"Well, keep the noise down. I have a headache."

"Me too," Tommy said.

I heard the elevator ding. Seconds later, Dad unlocked the door and entered.

He shut the door behind him, locked it, and said, "You guys go back to your room."

"Did you find him?" I asked.

"Find who?" my mother said.

"I'll explain later," he told her. "Now you boys go. Now."

He picked up the phone and dialed.

We walked to the hallway, but instead of going back to my room, I tucked myself against the wall far enough away so that Dad couldn't see me. I motioned with my hand for them to do the same. They quickly obeyed.

This is what we heard:

"Alem, this is Sanderson. I need you to call the local police and have them meet me at my building. Yes. It's urgent. I'll be standing near the playground area of the building. I'll need you to come right away to translate. I'll explain when you get here. No. Just you."

I heard him place the phone back on the receiver. We made a dash to my bedroom.

I left the door open. Dad entered.

"I'll be downstairs waiting for the police. First, tell me if any of you touched anything that might be evidence."

We looked at each other.

"What did you do?"

"Well, I sort of poked him with a stick to see if he was alive."

"Other than that. Anything? Who vomited?"

I was embarrassed to say.

"I did, Mr. Sanderson," Roddy said. "I got sick."

"Me too, Dad. Sorry."

"Nothing to be sorry about. I just need to know. I know Lenny has a diplomatic passport. Do you, Bill?"

"No sir. My dad's a teacher."

"Okay. You're going to need to tell your parents. There's nothing for you boys to worry about. Okay?"

We all nodded.

"Is it illegal to vomit on a crime scene?" Roddy asked.

"No, Bill—I've even seen police do that before. It's not illegal." He smiled.

"When did you see this kinda stuff before, Dad?"

"When I was in the military, Graham. Now you stay in the room here, unless you two have to go home."

"I can stay, sir," Lenny said.

"Me too."

"Okay then," Dad said and walked out.

We heard him say something to my mother, and a minute later the front door shut.

"Damn, they'll discover our fort for sure," Roddy said.

"Good thing I got my A&W bottle."

"That would have definitely been evidence," I said. "Let's go to the balcony but stay low so they don't spot us."

They followed me to the balcony. We crouched down and peered between the rails.

THIRTY-SIX

ad led Alem and the four uniformed police officers to the body. Two of the officers were in view when they turned the corner at the end of the wall. Several people were out on their balconies and along the road watching. Abu Fouad and the concierge were on the sidewalk next to one of the marked police cars. All I kept thinking about was how I'd have to lie to the police when they questioned us about finding the body. I knew that had to be a crime. Even my friends were in on the lie. They were protecting me. What made it worse was they were protecting me not from the murderer, but from my own father. From being grounded.

Dad came up later. We heard him in the living room talking to my mother.

She said, "Did you pick this godforsaken place because you knew there'd be a war and this kind of violence? It's an unsafe environment for the kids."

I turned the volume on the record player up so my friends wouldn't have to hear them fighting. They acted like it was nothing. Dad entered the room a few minutes later. He didn't complain that the volume was higher than normal, but I turned it down.

"The local police handle things a bit differently here. My statement to them was enough. They won't be needing to talk to any of you. The man more than likely got into a fight that got out of hand. You boys did the right thing by coming to me."

I thought about Abu Fouad and how I had run into his store first, but kept that from Dad. Abu Fouad hadn't understood a word I was saying anyway, so I felt it wasn't that important.

It was on our minds for days. We spied from our balconies and took notes of who we saw walking the area below the hill, but without my binoculars it was hard to see much of anyone. It still could have been something as simple as a fight gone bad, and the other man could have been from another country, even American. We liked to think it was something more, though. Something bigger, like spies. We didn't know what the hell we were doing or what we would do with the information we got. Playing detectives. That's all it was. When we were able to sneak out, we carried our notebooks, discreetly writing descriptions of those we considered suspicious, or of people we had not seen before. We'd even sit on the cinder-block wall behind the building that separated our building from the vacant lot and the demolished building on it. We'd sit at the edge by the road where we had a good vantage of the front of Abu Fouad's store. It was far enough from his store that he didn't shoo us off for loitering. He was surprisingly busy for such a small store. Mostly locals, and a few younger kids from the building.

We didn't go back to the fort. It felt off-limits, like our

sanctuary had been violated. We did occasionally bring it up, each story more embellished than the last and always ending with the possibility of *what if:*

What a madman was out there, looking for us because we knew?

What if we were in danger?

That became the new adventure.

When we weren't breaking curfew we hung out at one another's apartments, listening to music and making up war games where the bedrooms were the command centers and the balconies were the dugouts. Part of the fort was in our sights, but it was more like a stronghold that had been overrun.

We soon found ourselves going back to school. We'd meet in the early mornings just outside the village and walk to the campus together. My mother walked with us, but only to make sure Tommy got to school safely. She was obsessed with his safety. She was clearly unhappy in Beirut. She wanted to return to New York, stay with friends. They fought almost every night about it. I wanted to ask if they were going to get divorced. Oddly enough, it's not like I dreaded the possibility. My mother had been so distant from me for so long that it didn't feel like I had a mother at all. And it had all started after my sister's death; she couldn't let it go. As far as she was concerned it was all Dad's fault (and partly mine for surviving, or not being taken in her place).

One day at school while on recess, a group of older kids had pulled themselves up the wall and were sitting and hanging on it to look over the other side. Several had gathered. I was with Roddy, Lenny, and this nerdy kid Robert. We were standing around a grassy area tossing pocketknives at the ground to see who could make them stick the most. We folded the knives up, put them in our pockets, and went to the wall to see what the fuss was all about. We jumped to grab at the ledge and pull ourselves up.

Robert didn't make it.

"What's going on?" he kept yapping. "What's going on?"

About three blocks down a narrow road was the Corniche. Several tanks with accompanying soldiers were traveling south on the Corniche. Traffic was held at the far lane and restricted from moving. Pedestrians were on the seawall side, looking on like it was a parade. That's what we thought too. The curfew had been canceled, and the bombing had stopped some time ago, so maybe it was a parade because Israel had been unable to invade the south.

I asked my dad that evening after dinner.

"Nothing to worry about," he said. "More troops headed south as a show of force."

"Are we going to have another curfew?" I asked.

"It's nothing for you to be concerned about, Graham," was all he said.

THIRTY-SEVEN

It was Christmas break. My mother didn't believe in Christmas, but it was Dad's favorite holiday. For us, preparations and the holiday music started at least a month before. I knew it was rough on my mother because of Dani. Dad wasn't insensitive to that. Christmas was a source of comfort for him, I think. It certainly was for me. Being so close to Israel brought the Jewishness out in my mother. My mother wanted to put up Menorah candles in early December, but that turned into a huge fight. The candles worried Dad. Not because of Micheline—she was a Protestant. He feared what was outside the apartment, even though we never had any Lebanese families over, not even Alem. It was a chance he didn't want to take.

Dad decorated a large indoor palm with Christmas lights that he didn't forget to pack. I didn't believe in Santa Claus anymore, but Dad still made sure there were at least two presents for me from him. Probably more for Tommy's benefit than mine. My mother made sure I understood what the Jewish people felt about Christmas. Nothing negative, just that celebrating the birth of Jesus Christ was not something they believed in, because "we are still waiting for the Messiah."

The curfew had ended over two months ago, a couple of weeks after the bombings in Southern Lebanon. We were free to do what we wanted again, but Roddy, Lenny, and I stayed away from the fort. It wasn't all that long ago, really. I often wondered about the murderer, if he really was an American, maybe even someone Dad knew. He did not speak fluent Arabic—not that I did either, but I knew what the language was supposed to sound like coming from someone who was from Beirut. A couple of times I almost broke down and told Dad, but not enough time had passed to ease the fear of punishment. That was one of my primary fears in childhood. Not the temporary pain of a good ass-whipping, but having time or things taken away from me. Those were the most important things to me.

My parents had a huge fight on Christmas Eve. My mother threatened to leave and take Tommy with her.

"I want to go back to New York," I heard her say. "I am not comfortable in this situation anymore. It is not a good environment for Tommy to grow up in."

I thought that was odd; why didn't she mention taking *me*? I would have fought to stay, but that's not the point. It is something that stuck with me. I don't have much of a relationship now with my mother because of some of what I heard her say while she was with us.

"I have no freedom here."

"You have friends."

"Friends. Friends! For God's sake, they're nothing but their husband's wives. You'll never understand."

"No, I guess I won't."

Dad walked into their bedroom, noticed me standing in the hallway, and almost looked embarrassed. But he didn't say anything—just slammed the door to the bedroom, and that was that.

That was the first time I can remember when I did not look forward to Christmas morning.

I woke up early. Too early. Everyone else was still sleeping. Buster wasn't whining to go to the bathroom yet, so I stayed in bed and waited for the sun to rise.

I was still in bed when Dad knocked and entered.

"I thought you'd be up and about by now," he said.

"I got up before sunrise, fell back asleep."

"A little too excited, huh?"

"Yeah, I guess."

I couldn't tell him I was feeling low because they'd been fighting on Christmas Eve.

I went out in my pajamas and sat on the couch with Tommy to survey the presents under the palm. My mother was on the other side of the couch, reading a magazine.

She even smiled when she said, "Micheline is making pancakes and scrambled eggs."

"Yay!" Tommy exclaimed.

Dad took Buster out for a walk. We had a Christmas day routine: As bad as we wanted to tear open the presents, we'd have to wait, eat breakfast, then let my parents get dressed and Dad get the camera out. I was patient enough. It was Tommy they had to talk down.

Micheline had breakfast with us. It was technically her day off, but she had agreed to cook. (My mother was not a good cook—couldn't make toast without burning it.) After breakfast, Tommy, Buster, and I sat around the Christmas tree, while my mother and Micheline sat on the sofa. Dad distributed the presents, starting with the traditional Santa gifts, including one for Buster. We waited for him to go first, because Buster loved to rip open the paper. He did, and found a nice rubber chew toy inside, which he grabbed in his mouth and took to the other side of the room to chew on. It would not last more than an hour.

Tommy and I opened our Santa gifts and received the typical pajamas with Christmas patterns on them: mine had Snoopy dancing around his decorated doghouse, while Tommy's had Santas and elves. We quickly set them aside as Dad passed us the stockings to dump. To our great surprise, they were filled with an assortment of American candy; Tootsie Rolls, M&Ms, Snickers, and a large Hershey bar. I think I shrieked like a little girl. Tommy certainly did.

"I placed an order with a buddy of mine who returned from the States. I think those are what you like."

"Heck yeah!" I said.

Tommy jumped in, "Can I eat them now?"

"Not all of them," said my mother.

"Why don't you start with one or two?" Dad said.

I tore open a Snickers bar, didn't even worry about the other presents until I'd finished it.

My mother gave Micheline some nice skin lotion. I tried not to think about it. Dad gave her a nice card with a bonus check and two days off. She was really grateful, thanking them more than once.

Tommy was very happy with what he got. His little soldiers were replenished with more soldiers, weapons, and two tanks. Dad gave me my last gift. The box was heavy. I tore it open. It was a thick brown box that had another wooden box inside. The top of the second box bore a strange insignia and the words *Walther, LUFTPISTOL.* I nearly jumped off the floor. I unlatched the box and opened it.

"Is this a real gun?"

"What?" My mother said, sitting up from the sofa.

"It's a single-shot pellet pistol. A Walther LP53. Those round tins have pellets in them. The round grip over the front of the barrel is what you use to cock it down."

"You got him a pellet pistol?"

"Honey, he's ready for it, and can only use it when I'm around." He looked at me direct. "Understood?"

"Understood," I more than agreed.

"That's no fair," Tommy whispered.

"You're just a little kid," I told him.

"That's enough, or I'll store it away until I think you're ready."

"Sorry," I said. "Can I take it out?"

"Yes."

"That can't be safe," my mother said.

"I already checked it. It's not loaded. It's not like it shoots bullets. Just relax. Let the boy have his time."

She sat down, but I could tell how reluctant she was. I didn't care, though.

That Christmas turned out better than I could have ever anticipated.

There were strict rules: I could never take the pistol out of the box without Dad's supervision. "It is not a toy," he kept saying. If he ever found out I had—especially if I'd taken it outside or played around with it with my friends—he would take it away. I could live with the rules. All I cared about was that it was in my room, and it was all mine.

Dad said we'd go to the mountains with Alem soon and go over everything I would need to know.

"It's a target pistol and will prepare you for the real thing when you're ready."

The real thing. Damn.

I couldn't wait to tell Roddy and Lenny.

"Can I at least show it to Roddy and Lenny if I don't take it out of the box?"

"Yes. I can trust you with that."

That trust made me feel good. I would never betray it.

THIRTY-EIGHT

We left for the mountains with Alem early in the afternoon the next day. The Walther LP53 was closed up in its wooden box and sitting on my lap. Dad was driving. Alem was sitting in the passenger seat. I was in the rear seat behind him. All the windows were open. The temperature was in the sixties—a beautiful, cloudless day. The pole fishermen were at their reefs, some in small groups on one reef. The promenade along the Corniche was busy with pedestrians. I was watching them, trying to identify the tourists from the locals. Sort of a game.

I heard what sounded like a loud crack in the distance, then people started running. A well-dressed man had fallen on the sidewalk. People scattered around him, but three men leaned down like they were trying to figure out what had happened.

Traffic stopped ahead. Dad did too. He turned to me.

"Get down on the floor! Get on the floor!" he demanded.

I froze for a second, fixed on the fallen man.

Dad reached his right hand over the seat, put the palm of his hand over my head, and forced me down.

"Stay down," Dad said. Then, to Alem: "A shooting?"

"We must go now," Alem said.

I leaned up as much as I could without drawing attention to myself. Dad was looking over his left shoulder, honking the horn and trying to back up. I could feel that he bumped a car behind him. Horns honking more. I was pushed backward by the jolt. He looked forward again, turned sharply to the right. I felt the car bump twice as it went over the median strip.

I pushed myself up a bit more to look out the window. Dad and Alem were too busy to notice.

"Watch out there!" I heard Alem yelp.

Then two more heavy bumps as we made it to the other side of the road. The car accelerated faster than I'd ever felt before.

Dad looked back at me for a second, then back to the road.

"You okay?"

"Yeah. Yeah."

"Stay down."

"What's going on?" I asked.

"Just stay down."

"Quickest way out of here, Alem?"

"Make this next left."

Heard more honking, then felt another sharp turn. My knees hurt from being bounced around. Soon after the turn, Dad slowed down.

"An assassination, I think," Alem told my dad quietly.

THIRTY-NINE

Alem had left. We were in the elevator.

"No need to worry your mother about all this," Dad told me. His tone serious.

"I won't."

I was cradling the box that held my pellet pistol.

My mother and Tommy were not home. Neither was Micheline, but it was her day off, so she was probably uptown. Buster was jumping and licking at us.

Dad smacked him on the side of the face and said, "Down, boy."

He closed the blinds in the apartment, and then in all the bedrooms. I followed.

"Stay in your room for me, Graham. And stay away from the window."

"Where are you going?"

"Just going to make a call. I'm not going anywhere."

He walked out of my bedroom but left the door open.

When I heard him talking on the phone, I crept down the hallway, staying tight against the wall on the opposite side of the hallway.

"It appeared to be an assassination. Yes. Sounded like it came from a short distance. Probably set up at one of the hotels. Yes. Yes. See what the Israelis know. Right. Okay. Talk soon."

I quickly made my way back to my bedroom.

I never found out if that man died, so I couldn't count him as my second body.

Dad came back and said, "I want you to stay home today until we find out what this is all about."

"Not another curfew!"

"I'm sure it'll be nothing like that. A lot happens in countries like this, so nothing for us to worry about."

"Are they at war with the Israelis?"

"The Lebanese? No, of course not. Some bad people living in Lebanon don't like the Israelis, though. The Lebanese are good people, but not without their problems, like in the States."

Dad gave it to me in the simplest terms. I was too young to understand what was really going on with the PLO and Israel. I only knew that he knew what he was talking about, knew that what we'd seen was bad—someone had been killed, again—and that Dad's phone call made him sound like a spy, not some regular Foreign Service guy.

"Can my friends come over, though?"

"I can't speak for their parents, but if it's okay with them, it's okay with me."

"Cool."

Roddy brought over his record *America,* by America. "A Horse with No Name" was playing. Roddy was looking through my comics, found *The Hulk* and said as if to himself, "This is a good one." He was sitting at the edge of the bed near Lenny's feet, who was plopped down on the bed with his head resting on Buster's shoulder.

Lenny cradled Buster's head with his hands and bent up. "So was there a lot of blood?"

"We weren't close enough, and then my dad made me get down in the back of the car, so I couldn't see anything."

"Probably a head-shot, though," Lenny said. "Most assassinations are. Brain's probably splattered everywhere, even on people."

"Gross, man. You're sick."

"What's this song even about?" I asked. "Traveling on a horse with no name in the desert? It doesn't even make sense."

"It's just a song," Roddy said.

"Yeah, but it's a weird song."

"Not as weird as your Jethro music," Lenny said.

"Jethro *Tull*," I said.

"'Thick as a brick'? What the hell does *that* mean?"

"Your head," I said. "Your head is as thick as a brick."

Roddy laughed.

Lenny rose to his knees on the bed, then tackled Roddy so they both fell to the ground.

"My comic book! Watch it!"

It had fallen to the floor when Roddy was tackled. I quickly rescued it, set it on the dresser near the turntable, and piled myself on top of both of them.

FORTY

There were nine people at the Christmas party, mostly couples except for the man with the bullet hole in his face. Out of politeness, my dad had invited the Stankeys. Roddy's dad, John, wore bell-bottom jeans and an untucked button-down white shirt and sandals. His mother wore a loose-fitting sundress with flower patterns. They were different from all the others. Seemed carefree, smiling and dancing to the music. Dad's reel-to-reel was playing *Top of the Pops* music—all the early-seventies, top-of-the-chart music. Carly Simon's "You're So Vain" came on. We could hear from in my bedroom. Buster was doing what he did best—sleeping on the bed, his head on one of my pillows. We were hashing out a plot to spy on the men, who were in the den smoking cigars and drinking a lot of alcohol. I had told Lenny and Roddy about the man with a bullet hole in his cheek.

We exited through my sliding-glass door and snuck around to the other side. The sliding-glass door to the den was open to let the cigar smoke filter out. We all hunkered down on our bellies. We positioned our heads close enough to the opening into the den so that we could hear, but hopefully not be seen. Fortunately, with drunkenness came loud and boisterous conversation. Roddy's dad was the only one not smoking a cigarette, but he was drinking beer out of a bottle.

"Oh, I like this song," he said, but was not heard or maybe not paid attention to. He wasn't like the other men. I never told Roddy, though. He started singing along to "My Sweet Lord" by George Harrison. Dad looked at him with a sideways glance and a half smile.

I was sure Roddy's dad was the type who protested the Vietnam War. Even smoked pot. I didn't know much about such things when I was twelve. I did find out years later that a senior at ACS had been caught with hashish. Didn't matter that his dad was a diplomat. He was tossed in jail for eight months before a trial and eventually let out on parole. Based on that, I figured Mr. Stankey was probably not stupid enough to smoke weed in a country that did that sort of thing.

There was another man there. He was tall and thick. Had a shadow of a beard. He wore a navy-blue sport jacket over a green polo shirt that had a circular insignia on the left breast. It looked official. Lenny's dad was also there. The other men were sitting in the living-room area, talking to the wives. A couple was dancing. That looked funny—parents dancing. *Drunk* parents dancing. Mother even joined in on the dance, holding her martini glass over her head. She seemed happy, in her element, or just silly drunk.

The conversation in the den was boring for a while. They were talking politics. Nixon was the president, but my dad was talking about Lyndon Johnson and something having to do with the assassination of John F. Kennedy. He said he'd been at a party where Lyndon Johnson was and overheard Johnson say, "We don't need another cripple in the White House." I didn't understand, of course.

"He was right," said the man with the green polo shirt. "But not because of his back."

"Spineless," the man with a bullet hole in his face said.

"He did a lot for our country," said Roddy's dad. "More than you can say for Nixon." Then, saying he needed another beer, he walked out of the room.

"Maybe you should tell him the Kennedys were nothing but a bunch of criminals too, but they got away with it," the man with the green polo shirt said.

"They didn't really get away with it, did they?" the man with a bullet hole in his face said.

"But the dad did," the man with the green polo shirt returned.

"Stankey's a good guy, even if he does like the Kennedys," Dad said. "He found the old binoculars my son lost. Has to be good for something." He smiled.

"Your dad found my binoculars?" I asked Roddy quietly.

"I was going to tell you."

"You got me in a mess of trouble."

Roddy's dad returned with another beer. He leaned against the bookshelf near the reel-to-reel.

"Shh," Lenny said. "This is getting good."

"Anything new on Matni's murder?" Lenny's dad asked.

I looked at Roddy and Lenny with surprise and mouthed, *Matni*. Lenny put his finger up to hush me again.

"The local police here are worthless," Dad said. "I doubt seriously they'll ever find a suspect. But if they did, they're not sharing it with me."

"Matni?" Roddy's dad questioned. "You mean the dead man our kids found at the hill?"

"Yes," Dad said. "His last name was Matni. It's no secret that he was one of the locals who worked for the embassy on occasion. I told the police that."

"Do you think his murder was related to anything he was doing for the embassy?" Roddy's dad inquired.

"No. He wasn't involved in anything that'd get him killed. He was just a local go-to man."

"That you know of," Bullet Face said. "I keep saying it, but you can't trust these locals for shit."

Dad smiled. "Probably got himself killed over a woman. Alem has a good source at the police department. We'll see where it leads."

"Shame the kids had to see something like that," Roddy's dad said.

"I know," Dad said.

"You need anything from my end, let me know," Polo Shirt said.

"Thanks. I was CID in the Army. Might be fun to dip into a good investigation again."

"The government allows you to do that?" Roddy's dad asked.

Dad chuckled and the other men joined in like they'd just heard a good joke.

"What?" Roddy's dad said.

"You're looking at the U.S. Government right here," Polo Shirt said.

"Well, cheers, then," Roddy's dad said, lifting his bottle of beer.

They all hoisted a glass.

"I think I'll go see what my lovely wife is up to," Mr. Stankey said.

He raised his beer again and walked into the living room.

"Did we offend him?" Lenny's dad asked.

"He's a high-school teacher at ACS," Dad said. "Might take a little more than that to offend him."

"Wife looks like she used to be a hippie," Bullet Face said. "Probably has a nice bush under that skirt. I'd dive into that! 'Slippery when wet,' you know."

Polo Shirt and some of the other men chuckled. Dad didn't. I had no idea what Bullet Face was talking about.

"Oh man," Lenny whispered like he knew. Had a wide smile.

"What did he mean by that?" Roddy asked.

"Yeah, what'd he mean, Lenny?"

"Oh, you guys have a lot to learn."

"What?" I demanded in a low voice.

"Shh," Lenny said.

"Now you can answer Stankey's question," Polo Shirt began. "Do you think his murder was related to any intel he might have had?"

"All I know is he was providing good intelligence on guns going to the PLO. We never got information on who, though."

"Why would he be killed with a machete unless it was something personal?" Bullet Face asked. "And why so close to where you live?"

"That's what bothers me. Like I said, I don't think I can depend on the local police to figure this one out. But that's probably a good thing."

"You may be right there," Bullet Face said. "You never know where it might lead."

"Yeah, if it's our house, we'll do the cleaning," Dad said.

I couldn't imagine what he meant by that. What did *our house* have to do with it?

Dad took a healthy sip of scotch, set his glass down.

"You know, this whole Munich thing is far from finished," Dad changed the subject.

"How do you mean?" asked Lenny's dad.

"There'll be more retaliation—and soon, I'm sure. They didn't quite make the statement they wanted to make."

"I'm afraid you're probably right," Lenny's dad said.

Polo Shirt said, "The Mossad has a way of handling things."

"Your sources telling you anything?" Dad asked.

"Only what you probably already know," said Polo Shirt. "The PLO has always been in the south of Lebanon so they can easily attack Israel. They're not much of a concern to us here, although they are around."

"It's the Christian Militia we should worry about," Dad said. "There's a Palestinian refugee camp near my off-site office."

"And their ties, especially in some of the Druze villages, to the Soviet Union," said Bullet Face. "Where do you think they're getting all their weapons from?"

"I'd say we're in for some more trouble soon," Polo Shirt said.

The conversation turned back to politics, and Nixon.

We commando-crawled back to my room.

Most of the lights from inside the large apartments on the hill were on.

"Where are your binoc—oh, I forgot," Lenny laughed.

"That's not funny. You should have told me, Roddy. In fact, you should have told your dad you'll give them back to me. Now I'm gonna catch it from my dad. Big time."

"You should be happy my dad found them."

"Yeah," Lenny said. "At least the murderer doesn't have them." Lenny folded his arms on the railing, gazing out to the buildings on the hill. "Wish your binoculars were here right now," Lenny said. "We could check out those windows on the hill."

"Maybe see boobs," Roddy said.

"Boobies," Lenny laughed.

"Dang, that man worked for the embassy," I said. "What if the murderer works at the embassy too?"

"Maybe you should tell your dad the truth," Roddy said.

"Are you kidding?"

"I'm just saying."

"It's too late now. He'd send me off to military school for something like that."

"Yeah, my dad too," Lenny said.

"Remember, we're a team here. Right?"

They both nodded.

"Yeah, we're a team," Roddy said.

We all leaned on the railing. The hill was dark. Seemed threatening.

FORTY-ONE

My parents were still sleeping when I woke up. Tommy too. Micheline was in the kitchen, washing glassware.

"Mornin'," I said.

She jumped, almost dropped a glass.

"Oh, my! You startled me, boy. You're like a shadow sometimes."

"Sorry."

"There is cereal for breakfast, unless you wish to wait for your parents to wake. I will prepare eggs and pancakes then."

"I'll wait," I said. "I just came in so I could feed Buster."

I opened the pantry, found a can of dog food. Opened it and dropped it whole in his bowl. He gobbled it up in less time than it took me to open it. I walked to the living room. Buster stayed in the kitchen searching the floor for scraps. It was still early. I'd walk him later. He was good at holding it. The punishment was worse than the relief, I guess.

Dad was the first one up. He was in his pajamas. His hair mussed up.

"You're up early," he said.

"No, you slept late, Dad."

"I guess I did. In fact, I need some coffee. Want some?" he joked.

"No thanks."

He walked to the kitchen. I heard him say "Good morning" to Micheline. He walked back out with a cup of coffee in hand, followed by Buster.

He sat down in his chair near the archway to the den. Buster sat near his feet, staring at him. A look that meant it was time to go out. Dad ignored him. Buster still sat there, staring.

I was surprised to see my binoculars on the coffee table beside his chair. I didn't say anything. He must have noticed me looking at them, however, because he set his coffee cup on the stand, glanced at the binoculars, and slowly picked them up.

"You have anything to say about these?" he asked.

"You found my binoculars?"

"I didn't. Mr. Stankey brought them to the party last night and gave them to me. He said Roddy told him they belonged to you."

"His dad?" I asked as innocently as I could.

"Yes, he was walking their dog yesterday and said he found them near the wall by the hill. He saw the initials on them in English. What do you have to say about this?"

I already had in mind what I'd say, so it didn't take long. "I left them at the playground, and when I went back they were gone. I wanted to tell you, but I was afraid you'd get mad."

"You never hide anything from me. You know that."

"I know. I'm sorry, Dad. I tried to find them."

That was sort of the truth because I did go back to the fort. Dad was good at interview and interrogation, and I was an especially easy subject, so I had to be careful not to back myself into a corner with more lies. He set the binoculars back on the table.

"Can I have them back?"

"I don't know if you can be trusted with them."

"I can. Give me a second chance. You'll see."

He sipped his coffee, took a calculated moment to think about it.

"One more chance. You lose them again and I'll take the pellet pistol."

Damn, after hearing that I didn't want to take the chance of reclaiming them. I couldn't imagine being without the Walther. I had no choice, though. If I didn't take them, he'd know I wasn't ready for the responsibility.

"Okay," I said reluctantly.

"And you be sure to thank Mr. Stankey for returning them."

"I will."

FORTY-TWO

Christmas break was over too soon. I never did get to shoot the Walther pellet pistol. I had to stay later at school on that first day back because I was getting tutoring from Mr. Britcher, the math teacher. It was half an hour. It was the same day, every week, at the same time. When it was done, I went to my locker for my backpack and made my way home. It was about a fifteen-minute walk, mostly through neighborhoods with tall apartment buildings, but also a poorer area with beaten down shacks made of stone, cinder blocks from previously demolished buildings, and tin sheeting. Feral dogs roamed around, eating tossed chicken bones out of the gutters. I loved the smells. Always something baking or cooking. That overpowered the bad smells, but they were still there too, if you worked your nose hard enough. It charged the air you breathed. The villagers never messed with us, nor did they ever beg. It wasn't like the States.

I had to walk from one end to the other, through the center of the Druze village, to get to our building. They were better off than most of the other villages in the area. Like one big family. Generations, I thought.

Once through the village, I made my way toward the garage area. Large trash cans for the building were against the far side of the wall. Cars were not parked along that area. We rarely cut through there to get to the elevator because of the flies, feral cats, and rats the size of feral cats, but for some reason I did that day. Maybe events would have played out differently if I had stayed the course and walked along the dirt path under the balconies. Maybe not. Things probably just happen the way they're supposed to no matter what you do. I am sure I would have been jumped either way.

That's what happened. Toufique appeared from behind one of the pillars near the garbage can. He was holding a machete. He was alone. Had he been there waiting for me all this time, knowing it was my late day and so I would not be with a group of Americans, including Lenny and Roddy?

It was fast. He jumped toward me and swung the machete down. I lifted my left arm up to protect my head. Dumbest thing I ever did, but I didn't think to run back out of the way and keep running. That's what I should have done. It was like it wasn't real, and he was planning to scare me by stopping the machete just inches away. He wasn't playing, though: the machete cut into my upper arm, the blow so quick it knocked me to the ground, and Toufique lost his grip on the weapon. Trying to break my fall with my left hand, my wrist twisted and I heard a loud *pop* but felt no pain.

My left hand was now useless—so limp I knew my wrist was broken—and there was an odd feeling of pressure in my upper arm, like the elastic of a balloon, plus a burning sensation. I scooted backward along the concrete with my feet. I was not close to being fast enough. I felt blood gushing down my arm. When I saw it, I felt sick, but adrenaline must have kicked in because even though I thought I would pass out I didn't. I tried to push myself up with my right arm. I saw Toufique grab the machete and raise it again. I never understood what the nearness of death meant until that moment when he raised the machete to finish me off.

Then, out of nowhere, a white shroud blew over me, and a moment later I felt myself being lifted. It didn't feel real. It would always stay with me, but not as one moment. Rather as flashes of episodic moments—vivid, spasmodic, and deep-seated in my memory.

I woke up briefly in the ambulance. The siren. Remembered two EMTs at my side, speaking over each other in Arabic. Speaking fast, the driver driving faster. I woke up again on a gurney. One of those EMTs still by my side. An orderly or nurse pushing the gurney. Another man dressed in white pushed a gurney past me going the other direction. I saw a young Arab man on the gurney. He was positioned on his side, his mouth filled with bloodied gauze, with half of his tongue hanging out by what looked like a thin red sinew. He made weird, gagging sounds, like he was trying to tell me something. I was scared. He was pushed out of sight.

I blacked out.

I woke up again when I was in surgery. There were two nurses and a surgeon. I sat up. The surgeon was bent over my left arm. The nurse pushed my head back down.

I went out again.

When I woke up, I was alone in a yellow hospital room. The bright fluorescent lights burned my eyes at first. It took a bit for them to adjust. I felt funny. Funny good. Morphine. The bed was propped up, so I wasn't flat on my back. There was a cast from my left hand up my forearm to below my elbow. My upper arm was wrapped with gauze all the way to the shoulder. My dad was at the foot of the bed, talking to the surgeon. The surgeon, Dr. Naifeh, was Lebanese. Still remember the name clearly. He turned, saw that I was awake. Dad came to the side of the bed, said something, but I didn't understand. I only remember my eyelids feeling heavy. Too heavy to stay focused, so out I went. Again.

FORTY-THREE

Before I made detective, I had a foot beat on the 1600 and 1700 blocks of Columbia Road NW in DC. One of the Third District's heavy drug spots at that time, it was controlled mostly by Salvadorans. There were a couple of large apartment buildings, but it was primarily a business area. Years before gentrification took hold. I remember walking up to a small park at the intersection of 16th Street and Columbia Road. There was a young man at the park waving a machete around like he meant business. Some lookie-loos stood on the sidewalk, but the young man had cleared the park. I was in uniform, so it was hard not to make me for a cop. Young man didn't care. I kept my distance, called for backup. He must've heard me, because he charged me. Guess he figured he was going to get himself arrested, so why not try to take me out before my backup arrived? Never did find out. He looked whacked-out on PCP, though. I remember trying to calculate the number of feet between me and him as he ran toward me. I yelled out commands for him to stop. I had no cover. He got too close, so I shot him. He died on the scene.

He was the third man I ever saw dead up close. Had the same look in his eyes as the first. A shared experience.

My stay at the hospital was a blur. Had to have a couple of additional surgeries on my fractured wrist. There were stitches inside and outside my upper arm, but fortunately the blade hadn't reached the bone. There was pain. Dr. Naifeh told Dad that I would struggle with pain for a long while because of possible nerve damage to my upper arm.

The cast was uncomfortable at first. It itched. Had to take baths, not showers. The bathwater could be only about six inches deep. Dad wrapped the cast in plastic.

Lebanese authorities interviewed me briefly. I was interviewed again by a couple of men in suits from the embassy. I never saw Toufique again. All Dad said was I didn't ever have to worry about him. I don't know if he was arrested or killed.

Lenny was the first one to autograph the cast.

He wrote, *You'll have a great scar to brag about.*

Roddy wrote, *G-Man is the man—your buddy for life.*

When I returned to school, I was like a hero. Everyone, including seniors, signed my cast. Even girls who'd never given me the time of day. Everyone wanted to hear the story, but I didn't remember most of it. Just the attack. Later I remembered more about the white robe, like a man over me, then being lifted up. Dad said it was the man that kept the pigeons on the hill.

"You call him the Pigeon Man," he said.

FORTY-FOUR

He saved me. Knocked Toufique to the ground, then Toufique got up and ran away. The Pigeon Man tore his robe and used it to wrap my arm, then carried me to Abu Fouad's store and called an ambulance. My parents were notified when I was at the hospital.

Dad said he thanked the man, who gave his name as Azim Ali, which I thought was ironic. Dad even invited him over for dinner, but he politely declined.

Roddy and Lenny couldn't believe it. They didn't want to believe it. It was like killing the boogeyman. Every kid needs a boogeyman.

"He was probably gonna carry you to the pigeon shack and feed you to his carnivorous pigeons, but then maybe there were witnesses so he couldn't," Lenny said.

"And your dad invited him over for dinner?" Roddy asked.

"He saved my life."

"That's outta this world, man," said Lenny.

"Yeah, and my dad said I should go thank him."

"He's going to go up there with you, right?" Roddy asked. "Just in case."

"I don't know. Personally, I don't think he's who we think he is. According to what my dad said, he sounds pretty normal to me."

"He speak American?" Lenny asked.

"No, my dad used this guy, Alem, to translate for him."

"I don't know—those things we heard about him can't all be fake stories."

"People tell big stories sometimes," I said.

"I still don't know," Lenny said. "Don't go thinking he's your friend. You'll end up disappearing like all those others we heard about."

"I don't know. Big stories is all," I said.

"Still, you'd better be careful," Roddy insisted.

The cast I had was awkward. Even sitting was uncomfortable, especially on the toilet. Micheline had to cut my food up so I could eat it. Luckily, I was right-handed. I had Tommy do a lot of things for me, even things I could do for myself, like get a soda from the refrigerator. He got fed up with it after a while, but Dad told him he had to help out. I took advantage of it. My mother became more distant. It was like she was afraid to see me. Maybe it reminded her of Dani. My parents argued—fought more. Most of the time they didn't even bother to wait for us to leave the room or go to bed. Tommy cried once, and my mother scooped him up and locked themselves in the bedroom. Dad said she was having a hard time with everything, but she'd get over it.

After school I stayed in the apartment. My parents wouldn't let me go out. Not with Toufique still running loose. Lenny and Roddy would come by and visit. We'd listen to music, sometimes do our homework together.

That night before bed, I was going to the kitchen for a glass of milk. My parents were in the den. Micheline's door was propped open a bit. I peered in. Took a little too much time. Micheline appeared from the kitchen.

"You looking for me, boy? You need something?"

"No. I was just—I don't know..."

I hoofed it back to my room. Forgot about the milk.

When I slept, I had to prop my left arm on a pillow. It was difficult because I rolled around, usually fell asleep on my side. I was restricted to sleeping on my back now. Sometimes, I'd wake up in the middle of the night because of the pain or because my body had tried to roll. It was like there was a heavy weight on my arm, like someone pinning it down. When I found myself in that state of waking out of a dream, but not fully being awake, my mind would play tricks on me. That night it was Toufique on top of me, trying to cut my arm off with Dad's Army buck knife.

FORTY-FIVE

My parents had a terrible fight while we were eating dinner in the dining room. My mother dumped a bowl of salad, dressing and all, over his head. He stood from his chair and faced her. I thought he was going to deck her, but he just tossed his plate, spilling the food on the table. After that he picked up his glass of scotch, downed the rest, then hurled the glass against the wall, shattering it. It was dangerously close to Tommy. My mother jumped back, startled. Tommy and I did too. Tommy started to cry.

"Don't let the children step in the glass," he said with a scowl.

Salad leaves were dropping from his head and shoulders as he walked away.

Two days later, she left for New York with Tommy.

Micheline cried.

"She just needs a break," Dad told me.

"Are they coming back?"

"I'm sure they will soon."

Everything changed after she was gone. Dinners were consumed in the living room or wherever we felt like eating.

Dad started growing a beard. Micheline was in charge, and my dad told her to make sure I stayed inside. He was worried because of the general violence in the city.

Dad let me go over to Roddy's apartment for dinner on Saturday. His dad grilled hamburgers and hot dogs on a small grill on the kitchen balcony. At first I felt a bit awkward about the binoculars, and how his dad had come to find them. It was possible that the murderer had taken them from the fort and dumped them later. Still couldn't understand why, though. I thanked Mr. Stankey for returning them.

"I'm just happy I could find out who they belonged to," he said.

Roddy and I ate on rickety beach chairs on the seaward side of the balcony. His little mutt was begging for food—and so were a couple of pesky seagulls.

"Watch this," Roddy said.

He tossed a French fry out over the balcony. The two seagulls swooped for them. The one that didn't get it would fly after the one that did. When they were done, they'd fly back, perch on the balcony rail, and squawk for more. They were bold and unafraid. If you set your food down, they'd be sure to get a bit of it.

"Flying rats," Roddy said.

"I thought pigeons were flying rats."

"They're all flying rodents." He turned to me, still chewing his burger. "What did it feel like getting stabbed?"

"I don't remember."

"How could you not remember?"

"My dad said it's like a thing the brain does. Helps you cope with bad things that happen."

"Trauma," Roddy's dad said as he stepped out to the

balcony holding a bottle of beer. "It's a defense mechanism. Your mind avoiding conflict."

He shooed the seagulls away and said, "Flying rats. That must have been very scary, Graham."

"Yes sir, it was."

"None of that *sir* crap with me, Graham. My students call me Mr. Pete."

He took a sip of beer.

"Do you know if the authorities caught him yet?"

"No sir. I mean, Mr. Pete. My dad said his family is probably hiding him."

"Probably in some cave in the mountains," Roddy said.

"Doubt that very much, son. They're wealthy. I'm sure he's up north somewhere, in a nice, comfortable home. Don't worry though, Graham: he won't get away with it."

"I hope not. I can't go outside because of him maybe being out there."

"Speaking of outside—I know you boys were sneaking out during the curfew."

Roddy straightened in the chair, ready to speak.

"Don't worry," his dad said. "I'd be doing the same thing." He leaned his back against the balcony, took another gulp of beer. "Now tell me the truth. Are you boys getting into something that might provoke the locals, particularly Toufique or his family?"

"No, Dad! He started that fight. We were just trying to walk past them."

"What do you do out there all day?"

"Just explore. Look for lizards. Stuff like that."

"Nothing else? Getting into places you don't belong?"

"No, Dad."

Did he mean the hill? The fort? Did he know?

"I only ask because you never know. Some of these locals are damn idiots."

He smiled awkwardly.

"Well, I'll leave you boys to it, then. Beautiful day. Enjoy."

"Thanks, Dad."

"Happy you could come for dinner, Graham."

He shot us a quirky smile before walking back into the apartment.

"Wonder what Lenny's doing?" Roddy asked.

"I don't know."

I felt uncomfortable—like I wanted to jump from my chair but didn't know why. A silly thought, really, so I tried to shrug it off. He was a hippie, after all. A dad.

FORTY-SIX

I had a new cast over my hand and forearm. The doctor had to reset the bone and put pins in because the broken ends of the bone were not healing the way they should. Dad let me keep the old cast because of the signatures. Lenny and Roddy were the only ones to sign the new one. I decorated much of it with a black Magic Marker. Things like a peace sign, a heart with an arrow through it, and nonsensical swirly designs.

Toufique was in the wind. I heard nothing from Dad—only that I was still restricted. I was going stir-crazy. Micheline would check on me if I said I was going to Roddy's or Lenny's house, to make sure that's where I really was. She took my dad's direction seriously, as if her job depended on it. Maybe it did. Like I said, things changed when my mother left. I had not heard from them in the weeks since, not so much as a letter from Tommy. I knew my parents were getting divorced. I wondered if that meant Tommy would no longer be my little brother, or if I'd ever see him again.

Believe it or not, school was my only break from prison. It was like work release, and I looked forward to it. Spring break was close, and I was not looking forward to that. All the kids, specifically Roddy and Lenny, would be outside playing Kick the Can or hopping the reefs.

One night I was gazing out the bedroom window, thinking about a way to sneak out the next day. A 45 of The Archies, "Jingle Jangle," was playing on the stereo, a song I'd never admit to my friends that I liked. I noticed a group of men in dark clothing, their faces covered with what appeared to be ski masks, carrying semiautomatic weapons. They were running single file toward the Stinky Steps. I had watched them run halfway up when Dad jerked me away from the window by my shoulder.

"Get away from the window," he ordered.

"What's going on?"

He immediately pulled the curtains shut and walked me to the other side of my bed, away from the window.

"What are those men doing?"

"I need you to listen carefully. Stay away from the windows. In fact, you'll be sleeping in my bedroom. We're going to have a campout on the floor, except without sleeping bags."

"You never tell me what's going on."

"There's going to be some trouble tonight."

"What kind of trouble?" I instantly felt more frightened than before. Worse than seeing the man stabbed at the fort.

"It has to do with what happened at the Olympics. Remember?"

"There's going to be more bombing?"

"I don't know, but we'll be safe here."

"Then why do I have to stay away from the windows?"

"Son, a bullet can travel more than a mile. We're just playing it safe."

"What about Micheline? Is she going to camp with us?"

He looked at me funny.

"No. No, she'll be safe in her room. It's at the back. I'll help you with your pillows. You grab your top blanket."

"Can I bring my flashlight?"

"Yes."

It was no longer my parents' room. It was just my dad's room, barren of everything that had to do with my mother. We fixed up our sleeping spots on the floor beside his bed, away from the windows. Buster snuggled into a spot between us. Dad rested his hand on the top of his big head.

It wasn't long before shots broke the silence. Rapid-fire *pops* echoing in the distance.

"Is that uptown?" I asked.

"I believe that is where they were headed. Keep your head down."

"Is this what it was like in Korea?" I was still scared, but interested too.

"Aside from the warm blankets and comfortable floor, yes."

"And Buster."

"And Buster. He would have made a nice juicy steak."

"No! Really?"

"Just joking. He would have been the troop mascot. The North Koreans would have made steaks out of him, though."

"That's sick."

There was a loud explosion. I jerked up. Dad placed his hand on my shoulder. More gunfire after.

Imagining I was a soldier in a war, I wished I had my Walther to sleep with.

I stayed up most of the night, even long after the shooting stopped. It was like a storm, and I was just waiting for the next roll of thunder to crash over our heads. I don't remember what time I fell asleep, but early-morning light was seeping through the opening at the top of the curtains.

FORTY-SEVEN

Damn, another curfew," Roddy said.

"My pop said the Mossad snuck in on Zodiacs from a big boat right near here and ran up the steps. There was a huge gunfight on Hamra and a lot of PLO bad guys were killed."

"Damn," I said. "I was up all night listening to the gunshots. I slept on the floor with my dad."

"Yeah, I was on the floor too, but in my room," Lenny said.

"I was too."

"I didn't mind it. Actually liked sleeping on the floor. Hey, let's ask our parents if you guys can spend the night. We can camp on the floor in my bedroom."

"That sounds cool, unless your dad is gonna sleep with us."

"Ha! I doubt that," I said.

"Can your maid make us grilled cheese?" Lenny asked.

"She's not a maid," I said a bit too harshly.

"Touchy," said Lenny, smiling maliciously.

"What do you mean by that?"

"You're getting a little uptight is all."

"I'm not getting uptight. She's just not our maid. That's for rich people."

"Your nanny, then," Lenny said.

"I don't need a nanny. She's like a helper."

"Like a second mom," Roddy joked.

I agreed with him, but said instead, "She's just a helper. You want her to make those grilled-cheese sandwiches, or not?"

"Geez," Lenny said. "All right. A helper."

That night we fixed up the side of my bed with a sheet stretching from the bed to a couple of dining-room chairs Dad brought in. It made for a nice tent. We all had lost our sleeping bags at the river, and I was the only one with a new one, so they had to use spare blankets. The curtains were drawn, and Dad said going out on the balcony or opening the curtains was forbidden.

Lenny found The Archies still on the turntable.

He chuckled. "The Archies. That's little-kid stuff."

"Tommy was listening to that," I lied.

Roddy put it on. It didn't take more than a couple of seconds before he turned it up and we all danced and lip-synced to it. Oddly enough, they both knew the lyrics.

When it got dark outside, we turned off the bedroom lights and used our flashlights. We squirmed into our makeshift tent, our backs pushed to the bed, with Buster taking up most of the middle.

"I miss the fort," Roddy said.

"Me too."

"It's been enough time and nothing's happened. I say we take it over again," Lenny said.

"Are you kidding? That'd be stupid. The killer is probably still out there."

"You think so?" I asked. "I'm sure he didn't see me."

"Doesn't mean he's not looking for you."

"We can't just give up our fort like that," Lenny said.

"I'm not allowed to go out until they catch Toufique."

"Damn," Lenny said. "You have the killer *and* Toufique after you."

"*Damn* is right," I agreed.

"There has to be a reason he got killed," Lenny said.

"Money," I said.

"Or a girl. It's always a girl," Roddy said.

"Those are motives," I said. "But what if it's something bigger?"

"Like what?" Roddy asked.

"Like they're spies."

"C'mon—a spy wouldn't use a machete," Lenny said.

"Why not?"

"They'd use a gun. Maybe a Walther," I said.

"Walther?" Lenny said. "You don't even know what a Walther is."

"Yes I do."

"What's a Walther?" Roddy asked.

"A special pistol. Like mine."

"You have a Walther?" Roddy asked.

"No way, man."

"Wait here," I said and crawled out of the makeshift tent. "Don't look."

"What are you doing there?" Lenny asked.

"Just don't look."

I opened my closet door, reached up to the shelf, and pulled down the wooden box. I returned to the tent with it.

"I got this for Christmas."

"What is it?" Roddy asked.

I opened the box. Roddy gasped. Lenny's eyes widened. He was at a loss for words.

"It's a Walther pellet pistol, but made like the real thing."

I carefully took it from the box, held it like Dad taught me.

"Let me see it," Lenny cried.

"No. It's not a toy."

"Let me just hold it. I've shot real guns before."

I aimed it over Buster, toward the other side of the tent, closed my left eye, and acted like I meant business.

"A spy would use a gun like this," I said.

"That's not even a real gun, though."

"C'mon, let me hold it."

"Okay, but seriously, no goofing off. My dad'd kill me if he knew. Worse, he'd take it away for life."

"I'm not stupid," Lenny said.

I handed it to him. He held it in his right hand, pointed it out.

"Pow! That was a head-shot," he said. "Damn, it's heavy. Even feels like a real gun."

"It *is* a real gun. Walther made it. Now give it back."

He held it stretched out a little longer, acted like he was shooting it.

"C'mon now," I said and grabbed it from him.

"Let *me* see it now."

I handed it over to Roddy. He cradled it in his hands like it'd break.

"It's heavy."

I took it back from him, placed it in the box, and slid it under my pillow.

"We'll keep it here just in case."

"Just in case what?" Roddy asked.

"In case the killer comes for us," I said seriously.

FORTY-EIGHT

Toufique was caught late the next day.

I was settled on my bed, the makeshift tent still up on the floor from the night before, when Dad came in, sat at the end of the bed, and told me.

"He's in police custody."

"Are they going to let him out?"

"I seriously doubt that. You know what a *suspect* is, right?"

"Yeah—someone who might be guilty of another crime."

"Yes. The police strongly believe he's responsible for that other man's murder. He won't be going anywhere."

I was stunned. Never saw that coming.

"They do?"

"Yep. You won't have to worry about him anymore."

"He's a kid, though. They're not going to execute him?"

"That's not something you should worry about."

"But they can execute him for murder, right?"

"I'm sure they can. But like I said, you don't have to worry about things like that."

I knew Toufique was not the one who had killed the man, because the murderer was bigger and older and didn't speak fluent Arabic. I was sure he was from another country, possibly even American.

"Can they execute him for what he did to me?"

"Why are you worried whether he'll be executed or not? He did this to himself. You had nothing to do with it."

"It's not that. It's just that..."

"What, Graham?"

"He's not much older than me, is all."

"You're not at fault here, Graham."

That stuck with me. All I could think was what a terrible mess I had gotten myself into, and especially Toufique. I knew he should be punished for what he did to me, but certainly not for a murder I knew he didn't commit. Yet I was the only one who knew.

FORTY-NINE

I called Roddy and Lenny for a meeting, said it was an urgent matter. We met at Roddy's apartment, in his bedroom. We sat on the floor at the side of his bed, facing one another. The bedroom door was closed.

I filled them in on what Dad had told me.

"He didn't kill that man," I said.

"But he tried to kill *you*," Roddy said.

"I heard the penalty is by hanging," Lenny told us.

"You're not listening. I was there. It wasn't him. Yeah, he tried to kill me because of a stupid fight we had, but he didn't kill that man."

"How do you know it wasn't Toufique? You said you never saw his face," Lenny reminded me.

"The murderer was bigger—he was an adult. And didn't speak Arabic well. I don't think he was from this country."

"You have to tell your dad so he can tell the police," Roddy said.

"You do that, we'll all get in a heap of trouble," Lenny warned.

"I'm the one who lied, not you guys. I can't see any other way out of this."

"But we all said we found the body! We're in on the lie."

"You did find the body with *me*. I showed it to you. All I'd have to say is that I lied to you guys too because I didn't want to get you in on it. I was scared, or something. Which is almost true."

"I guess that might work," Lenny said.

"But isn't that a crime, what you did?"

"I don't know. I don't think so. And I can't just let him hang for something he didn't do."

"In this country they'll probably hang him for what he did to you," Lenny said.

"We don't know that for sure, but even then I can't let it go. I'd pay for it somehow. I know I would, because I'd let an innocent kid hang. And that's all he is—a kid. Can't be more than fifteen."

"Maybe a kid, but he woulda killed you if the Pigeon Man didn't stop him," Roddy said.

"The Pigeon Man. Who woulda figured?"

"Yeah, I know. I think about that a lot."

"You know, you can tell Roddy's dad first. He's a teacher and knows things. Maybe he can help."

"No," I said, feeling even more panicked. "That'd just be bringing someone else in on the mess."

"I'm gonna have to tell my dad at some point."

"Me too," Lenny said. "Last thing I need is him thinking I was lying."

"Let me tell my dad first, though."

"Wouldn't want to be in your shoes," Lenny said.

"I'll have to take the punishment. It's the only way."

"What if they let him out and he tries to kill you again?" Roddy asked.

"They can't just let him out. He's still guilty for what he did to me. Or can they?"

"I don't know," Roddy said. "Maybe they'll just cut off his right hand and let him out. They do things different here."

"Stop kidding. This is serious," I said.

"I'm not kidding, man. That's how they do things here."

"I've heard that too," Lenny said.

I stood up.

"I'm gonna tell my dad. He'll know what to do."

"This is gonna be something," Lenny said.

Buster greeted me at the door when I walked in. He followed me to the den. Dad was reading the *Sunday Times*. Buster kept licking at me, eager for my attention.

"Stop it, Buster," I said as I pushed his head away.

He sat on the floor as if offended.

"Dad, can we talk?"

"Of course."

He folded the newspaper and set it on his lap. Buster walked over to Dad and curled his big body at his feet. Dad patted him on the head.

"You're a good boy," he told Buster. Then, to me: "What's up?"

"I have to talk to you about something."

"Sounds serious. Maybe you should sit down."

I sat in the seat next to him. I didn't know where to begin.

"What's going on, Graham?"

"I need to tell you something."

"Okay. You already said that."

"I just . . ."

"Are you still worried about that Toufique character? Because I told you, you don't have to."

"I am sort of, though, because there's something else. Something you need to know. I didn't really tell you everything the way it happened."

"About the fight between you and that punk?"

"No, Dad—about the dead man."

"Dead man? You mean the man who was murdered?"

"Yeah...yes."

"What about him?"

"I sort of, umm...I sort of was there."

His look turned serious. He knew what I meant.

"You were there."

"When it happened. I was there when he was killed."

"You were *what*?"

"Just listen. Please."

"I'm listening."

"We have a fort, Dad. Me, Bill, and Lenny. We have a fort we built. Chameleon Fort. Sometimes we'd break curfew and go there."

I thought he'd blow up after I said that, but he listened quietly.

"We were all there that day, but Lenny and Bill left before it happened and I stayed, just playing spy with the binoculars. That's when the two men came up near the fort. I heard them fight and saw...and saw the man with the beard fall. It was right in front of me, but all the branches around the fort kept me hidden."

"You witnessed the murder?"

I had been saying that all along, but it's like it had just sunk in, like he hadn't fully understood until now. Didn't want to understand.

"Yeah—I mean, yes sir. I saw him get killed, but I didn't

see the man's face who did it. I only saw part of his body and heard him talking. I know for sure that it wasn't Toufique, Dad. He was an American."

"How do you know he was an American?"

"Because of what he said after he killed him."

"What did he say?"

"He said *Damn fool.*"

He was quiet. Sat there staring at me, like he was either trying to process everything or getting ready to belt me—or both.

"The man—he must have heard me move or something, because he stabbed the machete through the fort."

My dad's face tightened. Before he could say anything, I continued.

"I ran. I didn't look back. I just ran as fast as I could to the store for help, but Abu Fouad kicked me out. He didn't understand a word I was saying.

"You could have been killed."

"I know."

"Did the man chase you? Did he see you?"

"No, I don't think so. When I got out of the fort and around the wall to the road, I took off. When I left the store, I didn't see anyone."

"Graham, did the man see your face?"

"I don't know," I said. "I don't know how he could've."

"Did you see his face?"

"I told you, no."

"I need to make sure, Graham."

"I didn't, Dad. I only heard him and saw part of what he was wearing."

"What was he wearing?"

"Just that they were tan pants, like the kind you wear sometimes. They were clean."

"Anything about his voice that you can remember?"

"Not really, except I know he was an adult, and I think he was an American."

"Anything else you remember?"

"No. I'm sorry, Dad."

"You should have come to me," he said calmly.

"I was scared, Dad. What's going to happen?"

"I'll take care of everything."

"Will I be in trouble with the police?"

"No."

"I'm sorry."

"I'm not going to say it's okay, but I am proud of you for coming forward, even though it wasn't right away. You know you can trust me with everything?"

"I know, Dad. So what now?"

"I'll need to know where your fort is."

FIFTY

The curfew was extended. Not only was there mounting tension between Israel and the PLO, but also skirmishes between the Christian Militia and the Palestinians. I wasn't grounded, but I might as well have been. Dad called a couple of times a day to check in on me. The balcony was off-limits and the curtains were always closed. We slept on the floor, beside our beds. I'd hear occasional gunfire erupt day and night. Not like before, when there were also explosions.

Micheline was vigilant, and strict, which made it impossible to get away with anything. And about all I tried to get away with was sneaking out on the balcony. I didn't think about trying to break curfew and go outside the apartment building. That was the last thing on my mind. My life would be over if I got caught doing that. But life in Beirut, the most exciting place I had ever lived, became dull, fast. I even found myself missing Tommy. Not that we had ever played much, but just his presence would have been a break. Knowing someone else was there.

All that aside, telling Dad about the murder had been a huge relief. It was a burden I didn't like to carry on my own.

Hearing that he'd take care of everything was a comfort too. It made everything bearable.

I wasn't allowed to go over to Lenny's or Roddy's place, but they could, on occasion, visit me. It wasn't until a couple of days after we had first spoken of the murder and my telling my dad the truth that Roddy could come over for the first time. Lenny was grounded for breaking curfew and going to the fort. I screwed up there. I should have never put them in the fort with me, but I wasn't thinking straight. Lenny wasn't pissed. He was a soldier. When I spoke to him over the phone earlier, he said, "I got whipped good."

Roddy and I were huddled on the floor listening to Grand Funk Railroad. He had one of my *Crime Does Not Pay* comic books on his lap.

"Lenny's always getting himself whipped," Roddy said. "Gotta have a leather ass by now."

We both laughed.

"I shouldn't laugh," I said. "If it wasn't for me, you guys wouldn't have got in any trouble."

"Oh, I didn't get in any trouble. My dad just said something like *Boys will be boys.*"

"I got a serious warning. Dad said he was going to take care of everything, though."

"You're lucky."

"Why?"

"'Cause you have a dad that can take care of things like this. I don't think my dad'd know what to do."

"He's a teacher. He knows a lot."

"A lot about books and grammar, maybe."

"He'd probably let you get away with murder, though."

"Yeah. Probably."

A burst of gunfire broke out in the distance.

"Quick, get under the bed!" Roddy yelled.

I began to crawl under the bed. Roddy laughed.

"You were going to go under the bed."

"That was just a reaction. 'Sides, my dad said a bullet can travel for miles."

"A *magic* bullet, maybe."

"No. Seriously."

"I scared you silly."

"Did not, man. You won't be laughing when they have to dig a bullet outta your ass."

"Ha! Bullet in the ass. Give me another poop hole."

"That's gross, man."

"Think we'll ever be able to go back to Chameleon Fort?"

"I don't know. Don't know if I'd want to. Not the same now," I said. "Besides, the police know about it and are probably doing some kinda surveillance."

Dad and I had dinner in the living room on dinner trays. The silence was something I had become accustomed to. Dad didn't talk much, unless it involved scotch and a couple of tight friends. Politics, the war, and back-in-the-day stories were all out of my scope.

He never shared anything having to do with the murder investigation, aside from the occasional *They're getting close* or *It's looking good.* I always wondered who *they* were. Was it the police, or were *they* Dad's people? I liked to think Dad's people—Polo Shirt or Bullet Face, for example—were involved. They seemed like men who could take care of things. I always hoped they would come over again soon so I could eavesdrop on the conversations.

*   *   *

Buster woke me up late that night. He was on my bed, facing the door, growling a low, uneasy snarl. The hair between his shoulder blades was standing on end.

I sat up, looked toward the closed door, back to Buster.

"What is it, boy?"

He jumped off the bed and growled at the door, clearly wanting out. He had been protective in the past, but nothing like this. I was fearful of getting out of bed, but I had to let him out, so I worked up the courage and opened the door for him. He ran down the hallway toward the front door, where I could hear him whining.

I walked toward the front door. Micheline had heard him and was in the living room.

"Does he have to go to the bathroom?" she asked.

"I don't know."

His growl became louder, then he barked at the door, becoming increasingly agitated.

"What's going on here?" I heard Dad say.

He was in his pajamas, wiping the sleep from his eyes.

"Someone's out there, I think."

I tried to look through the peephole, but Dad pulled me away.

There were two men mumbling outside, talking to each other. It sounded like Arabic.

"Micheline, you and Graham go to the den."

Buster jumped at the door, emitting an unearthly kind of growl.

"Now!" he ordered.

Micheline grabbed me by the arm. I saw Dad run toward his bedroom. I wondered why he was running to his room.

We went to the den and sat on the floor against the far wall.

"What's going on?" I asked.

"Shh, stay down here with me."

I heard someone kick at the door. Hard. Buster went crazy, unlike anything I'd ever heard come from him. Another loud kick. Buster sounded demonic, like he wanted to murder whoever was on the other side.

"I have a gun," I heard Dad yell. *"Bunduqia! Bunduqia!"*

There was silence. Uncomfortable. I could see Micheline was scared. She held me by the arm tight. Too tight.

After a few minutes, maybe seconds, Buster had calmed, but I could hear him whimpering and snorting.

Dad appeared at the archway, gripping his .45 in his right hand. I realized what he had run to his bedroom for.

"Probably just a couple of drunks," he said calmly. "Forgot where they lived. You two stay here until I sort this out."

"Yes," Micheline assured him.

I knew that was not the truth. They had sounded nothing like drunks.

He walked back toward the front door. I heard him pat Buster and say, "Good boy—good boy." Then he was on the phone talking. I wanted to creep closer so I could hear, but Micheline still held me tight.

I slept in Dad's bed that night. Buster too. We used pillows to create a border between us because Dad said, "It'll be like a campout."

I woke up to the sound of Dad's voice. He was on the phone. The bedroom door was slightly ajar. Buster was still at the foot of the bed. I crept out, sat on the floor, and angled my ear toward the open door.

"That's a possibility," I heard him say. "Yes, I'd feel more comfortable having security outside until we know for sure. No. I didn't get a look. I'm not sure. It could have been they were afraid of our dog growling and barking at the door like a hound from hell, or they heard me say I had a gun. It's a strong door. Steel. That sounds good. Roger that." And he hung up the phone.

I scurried back to the bed and under the covers.

Dad opened the door to check on me. I closed my eyes and pretended to be sleeping. He shut the door.

FIFTY-ONE

Bullet Face was wearing a white short-sleeved shirt tucked into neatly pressed gray slacks. He was with another man in a tan suit, whose hair was cut high and tight like the military. I was in the living room holding Buster by the collar so he wouldn't try to jump all over them. Micheline was in the kitchen.

"That's a good dog, there," said Bullet Face.

"Sure as hell is," Dad said. "He showed his worth. So did my son, Graham."

"I didn't do anything," I said quietly.

"Hi there, Graham," said Bullet Face.

"Hello, sir."

Dad put his hand on the other man's shoulder and said, "Son, this is Captain Trugman. He works with me at the embassy."

"Young man," he said.

"Sir."

Captain Trugman knelt down.

"C'mere, boy," he said to Buster.

Dad nodded at me, so I let him go. Buster happily obeyed and went right up to the man, trying to lick his face.

"Such a good boy," he said squeezing Buster's cheeks like he was a little baby. "Such a good boy." He stood up afterward and Buster tried to jump on him.

"Down, boy," Dad said, but Buster didn't listen.

"That's all right. It's an old suit."

Micheline appeared from the kitchen.

"Micheline, would you mind making a fresh pot of coffee?" Dad asked.

"Of course," she said and walked back into the kitchen.

"Why don't we talk in the kitchen?" Dad said, turned to me after. "You can stay out here or go to your room, Graham, but stay off the balcony."

And the big boys, including Buster, walked into the kitchen. I decided on the living room. It was a better spot to listen in on the conversation. Micheline came out after making the coffee and went into her room. She left the door halfway open, making it harder for me to sneak by and eavesdrop. I walked toward the front door and cut back along the wall, though. I sat against the wall near the entrance to the kitchen.

"How are you holding up?" I heard Bullet Face ask.

"As well as can be expected. I'm glad she wasn't around for last night. Not that she hasn't had enough, but that would have really sent her over the edge. Giving her time. We'll see how it plays out."

"Well, you need a good divorce lawyer, give me a call."

"Might take you up on that."

"I'm sorry to hear you're going through all this on top of everything else," Captain Trugman said.

"Thank you, Don."

"I'll have two men stationed downstairs in a car," he said. "If they're doing their job, you shouldn't notice."

"No need for that."

"Don't be ridiculous," said Bullet Face. "They're diplomatic security. That's their job. And I'm sure they'd rather be doing this than sitting at a desk drinking bad embassy coffee."

"Your sources telling you anything yet?" Dad asked.

"Nothing about last night, but the murder might have to do with a weapons deal gone bad. Too bad, though. That's what made Matni a good source."

"And the local police?"

"This is beyond their scope," Trugman advised. "I have a couple of men on it too, since it's so close to your home and involves an embassy source."

"I still can't see how any of this would have to do with me. I've seen the man around but didn't work with him. I don't know how the two can be related."

"Your son?" Trugman suggested.

Damn, that put me right in it. Dad was silent.

"It's a small community," the captain continued. "We have to look at everything."

"Maybe talk to that punk Toufique again," Dad said.

"We did," Captain Trugman said. "He's just that—a local punk who thinks he can get away with anything because of his father's standing here. Trust me, he would have owned up by now if he had anything to do with anything. Maybe you should take some leave. Stay here with your kid."

"Agreed," said Bullet Face. "Or send him to his mother in the States."

"No. He's better off here with me."

I didn't understand what that meant at the time. Going to stay with my mother would be the last thing I'd want to do. I'd sacrifice my freedom here any day over having to do that. I later came to understand what he meant, though. It was an emotional thing. The thought of my parents getting divorced didn't hit me then. Everything else that was going on far outweighed that.

"Things are going to start heating up in this country," Bullet Face said. "The militia is already arming up. It's only a matter of time before it becomes a hot zone here."

"I know," Dad said. "Attacking the refugee camp was just the beginning."

"It'll be kids with guns soon," Trugman said. "Little hood-lums running around."

"Any chance that's what happened here last night?"

"I'm not going to say it hasn't happened," Trugman said.

"You still have your M1?" Bullet Face asked.

"Yes. I have it handy."

I had read about M1s and seen pictures of them. They used them in the Korean War. They were semiautomatic rifles. I wondered then how much danger we must be in for Dad to need a weapon like that. All I had was the Walther. I thought of my single-shot pellet pistol, in its fancy box inside my closet. I didn't stand a chance.

Micheline stepped out of her room. Startled me. She shot me a glare, then walked into the kitchen without saying a word.

"Anything else, Mr. Sanderson?"

"No thank you, Micheline. We'll finish off this pot of coffee."

She returned, shook her index finger at me like I was being bad. She went back into her room and shut the door all the way. I felt like we had an understanding. Made me feel good. I needed an ally.

As with most adult conversations, this one soon turned to politics. I got bored and retreated to my room.

The curtains were drawn. I turned on a light. It was still dreary. This was my life. But not for long.

FIFTY-TWO

Even though Dad was on leave, he spent a lot of time either on the phone or away from the apartment. Sometimes he'd be gone for hours. He gave Micheline a number to call at the embassy if there was an emergency. The men downstairs didn't stay long. Security at the embassy was heightened, so they had to return. I kept my Walther handy. Practiced aiming at objects on my dresser. But I never loaded it. That would be the end of the Walther if I got caught.

There was a lot of sporadic gunfire. Sometimes it sounded like it was coming from right behind the building or on top of the hill.

After dinner, Dad retired to the den with Buster. Buster was more than happy to follow him around now that Dad gave him attention. That night, Buster had become the protector—the *hound from hell*.

I joined Dad in the den, sat in the chair on the other side of the room. He was smoking a cigarette and sipping scotch. No magazine or newspaper in hand. Just sitting there.

"Come to join your old man?"

"Yeah, I guess."

He didn't correct me for saying *yeah*. Things were changing. The biggest change weighed heavy on my mind.

"Are you and Mom getting divorced?"

He didn't respond right away. Took a long drag from the cigarette. Exhaled a waft of smoke, like a plume from one of the bombs dropped in Southern Lebanon.

"I don't know, son."

"If you do, what'll happen to me and Tommy?"

"Don't worry about such things. We'll always be a family."

That wasn't an answer, merely an attempt at comfort. I didn't know it then, so I didn't pursue it.

"Why doesn't Captain Trugman wear a uniform?"

"I guess because he doesn't want to stand out. Some of his men do, though, but mostly on embassy grounds."

"Is he a Marine?"

"Yes, he is."

"Was he in the war with you?"

"No, he's too young—but he was in Vietnam."

"Were you in Vietnam?"

"Filled with questions tonight, aren't you? I was in Vietnam, but not as a soldier."

"Why were you there, then?"

He huffed out a laugh, sipped some scotch.

"Because the State Department sent me."

"Can I go over to Bill's tomorrow?"

"Have him come here."

"I really want to go there. Both his mom and dad will be home. Please."

"We'll see tomorrow."

"I really want to go."

"I know you do, and we'll see tomorrow. Now that's enough."

I knew not to push it, so I left it alone.

The next day, Dad allowed me to go to Roddy's after lunch. Roddy opened the door before I knocked.

"Heard the elevator," he said.

"You were spying through the peephole."

"That too."

His dad was in the living room talking on the phone. He was speaking in Arabic. Broken Arabic. He hung up the phone.

"Damn fool," he said.

It hit me like a sledgehammer in the gut. The way he spoke. What he said. Who he was. The murderer. I was frozen. Don't know for how long, but Roddy shoved me on the shoulder and shook me out of it.

"You want to go to my room?"

I was overcome with fear. Didn't know what to say.

"What's wrong with you, G-Man? Let's go to my room."

"Yeah, yeah. Okay."

His dad turned and waved at me. I must have looked damn silly staring at him blankly like that. I followed Roddy to his room.

He closed the door after I entered. Plopped on his bed. I stood there by the door.

"What's wrong with you?" he asked.

I wanted to tell him. How did I do that? I was sure it was the same voice. It was his tone, the pause, the struggle to find the right word in Arabic. Mostly, the way he spoke the words.

"I don't know. Just feeling a little weird."

"What do you mean, *weird*?"

"I don't know." I chewed my lip, looked away. "I don't know."

"Whatever. You wanna listen to some music?"

"Sure."

He put on a record. It was Velvet Underground. I didn't know who they were, but I liked them.

"This is my dad's record. It's pretty cool for being the kinda music your parents listen to."

"Yeah, they're cool."

I was still standing at the door, thinking about what to say so I could leave. I had to tell Dad.

"You're starting to freak me out standing there like that."

"Sorry."

I sat on the chair at his small work desk. For a work desk, it was awfully neat. Most of his schoolbooks were stacked one on top of the other against the wall.

"My dad just told me we're going to have to go to summer school to make up for all the curfew days."

"Summer school. Damn."

"Yeah, it's a real pisser."

"I didn't know your dad spoke Arabic."

"Yeah, he has Lebanese friends. We've lived here for three years. Why?"

"I gotta tell you something, but you have to promise you won't freak out."

"What? I won't freak out. I promise."

"Your dad. I'm sure he was the man at the fort."

"What do you mean? When?"

"The man I heard when I was at the fort."

"You mean the murderer?"

"Yes."

"That's not even funny."

"I'm serious, Roddy. They sound exactly alike. He just said *Damn fool,* and that's what the murderer said. I'm sure of it."

"You're crazy. And if you're messing around with me, it's not funny."

"I'm not messing with you. This is for real."

"You honestly think my dad is the murderer?"

The door opened right after he said that. It was his dad. He poked his head in.

"I'm a murderer?" he questioned with a bit of a smile.

"We were just messing around," I told him.

Roddy looked pissed. Glared at me with squinting eyes.

"I have to go."

"You just got here, Graham."

"I forgot to take Buster out for a walk. I have to go now." And I brushed past him, down the hallway to the front door. It was unlocked so I ran up the stairs to the eighth floor.

FIFTY-THREE

Dad was in the living room, reclined on the sofa. He was napping.

"Don't wake your father up," Micheline whispered.

"It's urgent. I have to talk to him."

"Let him rest, Graham. Nothing is so urgent it can't wait."

"This is," I said. "Dad." I called out to him.

He woke up suddenly.

"What? Graham? What time is it?" He looked at his wristwatch. "I thought you were at your friend's."

"Dad, we need to talk. This is really important."

"I'm sorry, Mr. Sanderson—I tried."

"That's okay, Micheline."

He pushed himself up to a sitting position. Micheline entered her room, closed the door halfway.

"What's so important you had to wake me from a good nap?"

"I know who the murderer is."

"The murderer? How could you know that?"

"When I got to Roddy's house, I heard his dad on the phone. He was talking in Arabic. He sounded exactly like the man at the fort. At the end he also said *Damn fool,* just like the murderer said it. It's him. It's Mr. Stankey."

"Don't be ridiculous."

"I swear, Dad. I know it's him. It's the same voice. You have to believe me."

"Calm yourself and sit down."

I sat on the chair next to the sofa.

"I'm fairly certain that Mr. Stankey is not the type of man who would murder someone."

"Why won't you believe me? It's him. I know it is."

"I believe you, Graham. I believe you think he is. What is it about his voice that stands out?"

"It's just the same exact voice. That's all. The way he speaks an Arabic word, like someone who isn't from here."

"And why now? You've heard him speak before?"

"Never in Arabic. It's the way he speaks Arabic, Dad. Also, he found my binoculars," I said, not realizing 'til after that I had screwed up in a lie.

"What do the binoculars have to do with anything?"

"Well, I sort of didn't tell the truth about where I left them."

"Where *did* you leave them?"

"I left them in the fort after I ran away. After the murder. I was afraid to tell you."

"Graham," he said like he was about to set punishment.

"I'm sorry, Dad. I wasn't thinking straight. You have to call the police."

"We're not going to call the police. They do things differently here, and that would put his life in jeopardy. He's an American."

"What are you going to do?"

"Are you sure it isn't because he returned your binoculars?

All this time and you're working it up in your head? He said he found them near the wall. They could have been dropped there by someone else."

"No. It's not only because of that. It's because I recognized the voice."

"I think you're under a lot of stress."

"I am not. It's him, dammit!"

Dad straightened up on the sofa.

"I'm going to forgive that this one time because I know you're excited."

"But I'm telling the truth."

"Graham, it's too late to do anything now. I'll investigate it tomorrow. I'll check into him through someone I know at the embassy. Okay?"

"It's not that late."

"Tomorrow. That's final."

"I think he knows I know, though."

"What did you tell him?"

"I didn't tell him anything, but he overheard me talking to Bill about it."

"You told your friend you think his dad is a murderer?"

"Well, yeah. I think he should know, don't you?"

"Did his dad say anything to you?"

"No. Not really."

"Did you say anything to him?"

"Just that I forgot I had to walk Buster. Then I left."

"You don't have to worry about Mr. Stankey. I can certainly take care of him. I want you to calm down now and let me take it from here. Okay?"

"Then you believe me?"

"I believe you believe it."

"That's not the same thing. You never believe me."

"I believe you. Enough now. And you never lie to me again. Understood?"

"Yes."

"Good."

"Can I sleep in your bedroom tonight?"

"Yes. Like a campout."

The doorbell rang. I nearly jumped out of my seat. Buster ran to the door, barking, but nothing like before. Micheline stepped out of her room to answer.

"Let me get the door, Micheline. Thank you."

She smiled, walked back into her room. Dad went to the door but didn't look through the peephole. He patted Buster on the head.

"Quiet down, boy."

He obeyed.

"Who is it?"

"John Stankey."

FIFTY-FOUR

He looked through the peephole, turned to me after and said, "Go to your room, Graham. Take Buster with you."

"Why?"

"Because I want to talk to him in private."

"I want to stay, though."

"Go to your room now."

I pushed myself up and walked to the hallway, but instead of going to my room I stood near the archway with my back against the wall, leaning enough so I could hold Buster's collar.

Dad stepped into the hallway, saw me against the wall.

"I know your tricks. Take Buster to your room. Now."

"Man," I whimpered.

I led Buster to my room.

I patted the bed for him to come up. He leaped up, twirled around a couple of times, and fell to a resting position. I was amazed at how such a big dog could curl into such a small, fetus-like position.

I always thought I was good with my eavesdropping/surveillance techniques, but obviously Dad was better. He had said *Take Buster to your room,* but nothing about my having to stay there. I took that as an invitation to return. I would give it a bit of time, though. I looked at my Seiko wristwatch. Five minutes should be enough.

I returned to the wall near the archway, closer to the opening than before. I crouched down. It sounded like they were in the living room. I carefully peeked out. Dad was sitting on the sofa near the pillow his head had been resting on earlier. Mr. Stankey was in the chair next to the sofa. I could see my dad clearly, but only the left side of Mr. Stankey.

"Yes, Bill is upset with what he said, but I'm sure it's just a misunderstanding."

"He's been through a lot recently. I don't want this to get blown out of proportion."

"I can't imagine all that he's been through—witnessing that murder, then the incident with Toufique."

"He *has* been through a lot."

"When does the cast come off, by the way?"

"He goes back to the doctor in a couple of weeks. We'll see."

"And the laceration is healing well?"

"Yes. Stitches will stay in for a while longer."

"I'm sorry to hear about your wife and younger son having to leave the country."

"Word gets around here."

"Small community. How you holding up? Anything we can do to help?"

"I'll be fine. Thanks for asking. Tell me, John, why do you think my son would think something like that?"

"I was hoping you could answer that."

"I can only say he believes it."

"All that matters is whether you believe it or not."

"My son doesn't lie, but like I said, he's been through a lot."

"I'm a high-school teacher. I know how teenagers can be."

"He's not quite a teenager yet."

"Trust me, twelve years old—you're a teenager."

"What exactly did he tell Bill?"

"Bill only told me that they fought briefly because Graham accused me of being the murderer. Bill said he thought he was joking, but Graham insisted he wasn't. Kids sometimes don't understand the impact words can have. I know all too well what an accusation can lead to. I'm not worried about this, of course, but there are teachers who have lost their jobs or been reassigned after certain allegations of misconduct."

"Are you one of them?"

"Of course not."

"We'll keep this in-house then."

"Is that a government term? *In-house*?"

"Maybe a little."

"I have to tell you, I don't understand where this is coming from, especially after all this time has passed."

"I don't either, but I'm happy you stopped by so we can figure it out."

"So how *do* we sort this out?"

"Well, did you kill him?"

I leaned closer, thinking *Damn—he's asked him direct like that!*

Mr. Stankey laughed. Then, in a serious tone he said, "Of course not."

"How long have you and your family been living here?"

"This will be my third year at ACS."

"It's a good school?"

"One of the best."

"I apologize we didn't get around to talking much at the party. I would have liked to get to know you better. After all, our sons are best friends."

"Let's hope they can stay best friends. Bill is upset, and he doesn't get over things easily."

"Friends always have tiffs."

"I wouldn't exactly call this a tiff. Think about how it would feel if this were turned around, and it was you."

"Honestly, I wouldn't give it much thought. If I didn't do it, that is."

"You're saying I'm giving it too much thought?"

"Not at all. I was speaking of me. What do you teach at ACS, by the way?"

"English."

"You said high school?"

"Yes."

"We won't be here long enough for Graham to take your class. It's usually just a three-year assignment, and that would put him in ninth grade before we leave. I don't even know if we'll be here that long. Depends on what happens here."

"Any information you can share?"

"Nothing you probably don't already know. I do think Lebanon is headed for another civil war."

"Really?"

"All the different factions, and a lot of unrest."

"This country has had its share of wars. I do love it here, though."

"It is beautiful. Do you have many Lebanese friends?"

"Most of my friends are Lebanese. French, too."

"You speak French?"

"Better than I do Arabic. It was my minor in college. I always thought we'd settle there, but it's just so damn expensive."

"No teaching positions?"

"I've put in for a couple, but was never chosen. I do like it here. I'm not complaining. Listen, I really am enjoying our chat, but do you think it might be a good idea if we talk to your son about all this?"

"I'd rather not put him through any more unnecessary stress. Would you like some coffee? Tea, maybe?"

"No thank you, I'm fine. But don't you think under the circumstances it's important to have him here? I don't see any other way of getting to the bottom of this."

Last thing I wanted was to go out there. I was uncomfortable around Mr. Stankey. It was sudden, like Spidey sense.

"I'm quite comfortable with just the two of us talking. You're an interesting man. I think there's more to you than teaching high school English."

"What makes you say that?"

"I get the impression you've been around. Where did you get your education?"

"UCLA."

"Great university. I'm a simple Minnesota State guy."

"Nothing wrong with that university. What did you major in?"

"Believe it or not, criminology. After Korea, I did a brief stint as a special agent with the Federal Bureau of Investigation."

"That's a leap to becoming a Foreign Service Officer."

"Not really. The test was harder. It's just another government agency."

"I've been here long enough to know better than to ask what it is you do at the embassy."

"I just collect information, that's all. Nothing of real importance."

"So it's not a cover for the CIA."

"Hardly."

"That's too bad. I was hoping to have a friend in the CIA."

"Sorry to disappoint you."

"Just joking, of course."

"I know. I have to be honest, John: I believe my son."

"That I killed that man? You can't be serious?"

"He's scared. There has to be something to it."

"He's a twelve-year-old—a confused kid."

"I wouldn't call him *confused*. I'd say he's certain."

"Oh, for God's sake—this is ridiculous! And I thought we were going to clear this whole thing up. Is it because I returned the binoculars?"

There was a moment of silence. Looking back, I know Stankey screwed up bad. Looking back, I realize he wasn't all that smart.

"Why would you think the binoculars have anything to do with it?"

"I don't know. I found them and returned them—maybe he had them on him at the time? That could be how he witnessed the murder."

"Didn't you say you found them along the wall, off the road?"

"Yes."

"From that position he wouldn't have been able to see anything, let alone hear your voice."

"My voice? Now you're trying to trick me. Who the hell do you think you are, Sanderson?"

"Just a concerned dad. I wouldn't give a shit if you killed

the man. He wasn't an American. If he was, you'd be at the embassy for questioning."

"Based on what a child said? Hearing someone who *sounded* like me? I seriously doubt that."

"I could easily have that done. If the victim was an American, that is. Shit, in this country people have been arrested for less."

"Identifying someone by voice? I hardly think so—and I don't appreciate being threatened."

"I'm not threatening you. I don't want to have to take this to the next level, is all."

"This is absolutely ridiculous."

"Where did you really find the binoculars?"

"I already told you."

"I find it hard to believe that the suspect would have disposed of them there. Why would he do that?"

"You were the criminology major. You tell me?"

"I don't think he did. I think you found them right where Graham left them."

"I found them exactly where I said I found them. I don't have a clue where he said he left them. And even if I did find them where he left them, that wouldn't make me the murderer."

"I'm not comfortable having this conversation in my apartment anymore. I think I'll just give the information I have to the police—let them question my son, then you."

"I don't believe I'm hearing this. Your son is mistaken—and you'd ruin my life, my family, based on that?"

"Be honest with me, then. I can keep this in-house, possibly even protect you."

"*Protect* me? That's a bunch of bullshit and you know it.

You're trying to trick me again. Who are you, anyway? What authority do you have?"

"I have the authority to keep you out of the hands of the local police. I mean, there must be a reason for killing that Arab man. And I'm going to be honest with you, John: I know the suspect was an American. Because he said *Damn fool,* just like an American."

"That still doesn't mean he was me."

"Let me help you, John—help your family."

After a long pause, he said, "I don't know if I trust you."

FIFTY-FIVE

The best interrogation is when it doesn't feel like an interrogation. There's a calmness, and within that calmness there's the ability to find something about the subject that you can associate yourself with. That's when you have them. Yet another thing that stuck with me. You won't make it far as a homicide detective if you don't have those skills. Casually breaking someone down is deeply satisfying.

"You know, Sanderson," Mr. Stankey said, "contrary to what you might think about me, you should know that I did my time in Vietnam, and I know a spook when I see one. You're all the same—thinking your shit doesn't stink and you can get away with anything. Hell, how many people have you killed? Can you count them?"

"I'm not a spy. And killing someone is nothing to be proud of, but sometimes it has to be done, especially in war."

"Sometimes *out* of war too, right?"

"Yes. Sometimes it's necessary."

"What if I told you I might have information that could be very useful to you?"

"Are you really just a high-school teacher?"

"Yes, I really am, but I have outside interests to compensate for the shit pay I get. I still want to move to Paris with my family."

"No reason that can't happen."

"Lot of reasons that can't happen. You might be one of them."

"No, I'm not one of them, John. As silly as it sounds, I want to help you because our sons are best friends. That changes things. And I don't think you're a bad man, just caught up in something that is. And I think you want out."

"I know certain people who would be of great interest to an agency such as the CIA."

"What kind of people?"

"People who supply guns to terrorists—not just here, but in other countries. Very bad people. I met one of them in Vietnam. A Frenchman."

"Do you know who tried to break into my apartment?"

"I heard about that. We had nothing to do with that. The streets are teeming with gangs—kids armed with guns working with the militia. Maybe Toufique was their friend, I don't know."

"How would they know where I live?"

"My God, Sanderson. Abu Fouad is as dirty as they come. Maybe he was behind it. I don't know for sure. And we'll consider that information a freebie."

"Do any of these terrorists, including Abu Fouad, want to hurt Americans?"

"The other factions they supply guns to want to do that. Abu Fouad isn't one of those, but he'll stash them for you."

"I need more. Specifics. Then maybe I can go to someone I know at the embassy."

"Don't trust everyone at the embassy."

"Give me names."

"I don't have the names, only faces. But the Frenchman—and a couple others I work with—do. That's all I'm going to say. You make that call, but I'm not giving anything else until I talk to them direct. I want protection for me and my family. I want to talk to that person here. Face-to-face."

"Why did you kill that man?"

"That man means nothing. He was working his own deals. I'm not going to say anymore. Make that call."

I shouldn't have been looking. I shouldn't have seen it, but I saw my Dad pull his .38 out from under the sofa cushion. He pointed it at Mr. Stankey, who sputtered something unclear.

"Ever since that night they tried to bust in here, I've kept a gun handy. Never figured I'd have to pull it out for something like this. Now before I make that call, I need to make sure you're clean."

Dad stood up, faced Mr. Stankey.

"Stand up and lift your shirt."

"I don't carry a gun, just move them."

"Stand up, John, or it ends here."

He stood up. Dad stepped back.

"Now lift you shirt."

I watched him lift his shirt.

"Turn all the way around, John."

He did.

"Now face the wall, hands in the air."

Dad moved to pat him down, from the ankles up.

"Okay, you can sit down."

Dad lowered his gun but kept it at his side.

"I'll make that call now."

I got up and ran to my room just in case he could see me.

FIFTY-SIX

I couldn't believe it. Roddy's dad, a murderer, a gunrunner, a seriously bad guy with a laid-back lifestyle. And Dad, pulling a gun on him like that. What would Roddy think? I was pumped with adrenaline.

Buster started barking when the doorbell rang. I clenched his snout with my hand to muffle his yapping.

"Quiet, boy."

Someone knocked on my door.

"Come in."

Micheline entered, closed the door behind her.

"Your father said I should stay in here with you for his meeting."

"What? Why?"

"Because your father wants me here. I'm not good company for you?"

"No, it's not that."

"I'll sit right here at your worktable."

She sat on the wooden chair, positioned it so it faced me at the edge of the bed.

"Or if you would rather, I could face the wall so you can pretend I'm not here." She smiled.

"No. That's okay."

"You continue what you do. I will sit here quiet."

"I'm not doing anything."

"You can read."

"I want to go in the hallway. You can wait here."

"No, your father said you should stay with me."

"Just down the hallway. It's not like I'm going outside. You can watch me from the door if you want."

"So you can be like a spy on your father? I think not."

"It's no big deal. I do it all the time."

"Your father said we stay here. You obey your father."

"C'mon, Micheline. I'm bored. I'll be quiet. He won't even know."

"Graham, we do what your father asks."

"But it's really important. They're here because of me."

"Because of you? Don't be silly."

"They are."

"Why, then?"

"They just are. I can't say why."

"Graham, you are like family to me. You can tell me."

I hesitated to say.

"I am like your much-older sister."

"How old are you?"

"Shame. You never ask a girl her age."

"Why? What's the big deal?"

"You don't. That is all. It is impolite, and you will know why soon enough."

"I don't think it's a big deal. You know *my* age."

"So why is this about you?"

"Because I told my dad Mr. Stankey killed that man."

"Don't be silly. You are making this up."

"It's the truth. That's why I have to go out and listen. They won't see me."

"You can talk to your father after. I am sure your father called the police. That is why he wants us to stay in here."

"Man," I said like a whine. "My real sister would have gone out there with me."

"I am *like* your real sister, and I obey your father."

"Dani would definitely have gone out with me if she were here."

"You mean you do have a sister?"

"I did, but she died in a car accident."

"Oh, I am so sorry, child."

"It was a long time ago."

"Still, there must be pain. We can talk if you'd like."

I just stared at her, not knowing what to say.

I fell back on the bed, feet dangling off the edge, and stared angrily at the ceiling.

"You are my only family now, Graham."

I turned to my side to face her. Her skirt was up to her knees from sitting down. I rolled back to my original position.

"You don't have brothers or sisters?"

"No. I was the only child."

"Where are your parents?"

"They are in Africa somewhere."

"You don't talk to them?"

"So many questions."

"I'm just talking."

"Yes, but some things we like to keep private. You have things you don't want to talk about, yes?"

"I guess."

"And I would not expect you to tell me either."

"Okay, I get it. How about you let me go out there for five minutes? You can time it."

"No."

I could have just gone out there. What would she do? Grab me and hold me against my will? I didn't think so, but for some reason I listened to her. Maybe it was because of what she said about being alone. Maybe it was because of that time I saw her putting oil on her legs. I tried not to think about it.

FIFTY-SEVEN

Not going out there was killing me. I decided to sit up, but before I could make my move a gunshot rang out from the living-room area. I jumped out of my seat. Micheline shrieked and stood up from the chair. Buster jumped off the bed and ran to the bedroom door, barking. I knew it was a gunshot because of the time Dad took me to the mountains to shoot.

"Get down behind the bed!" Micheline cried.

Buster kept barking at the door. I couldn't stay there. I had to know what was going on. I ran to my closet, reached up to the shelf and grabbed the box that contained my Walther.

"What are you doing? Get behind the bed *now*!"

She grabbed me by the arm, but I tugged away.

"*You* get behind the bed. I have to see if Dad is okay."

"No. You listen to me."

I quickly placed the box on the floor, opened it, and took the pistol out. I heard Micheline gasp and say something unintelligible. I twisted the tin container and grabbed a handful of pellets, stuck them in my pocket. I cocked the barrel down, loaded a single pellet in the chamber, and closed it with a click.

"Hold Buster by the collar. Don't let him out."

"Graham. Graham, please listen."

"Hold Buster," I demanded.

She grabbed him by the collar. I opened the door, stepped out, and shut it behind me. I heard it open again.

"Come back here, Graham," she whispered loud enough for me to hear.

I moved as fast as possible to the archway, staying close to the wall. I peeked out. Dad and Bullet Face were sitting together on the sofa. Another man, Captain Trugman, was pointing a revolver at them. It looked like the one Dad owned. He had another weapon holstered at his right side. Mr. Stankey was limp on the chair and not moving. I could see only the left side of him, but the wall behind him had blood spatter on it.

"Where's that damn dog?" Trugman asked.

"Safely locked in a room," Dad said quietly.

"I always had an out, but never figured I'd have to use it so soon. The last thing I want to do is shoot the two of you. Stankey was a worthless piece of shit. We already had plans for him. If I didn't shoot him, the Mossad would have eventually caught up to him and done the job for us. He wasn't smart about business. But here's how it's going to work: you shot him with your revolver in self-defense. I have another weapon I can put on him. Then you're going to let me walk out of here. Simple. Keep it that way and we won't have a problem. Understood?"

"Clearly," Bullet Face said.

"Yes," said Dad.

Next thing I heard was Buster barking louder. I turned and saw he was running toward me, with Micheline after him. I tried to grab him with my good hand, but he broke past me and streaked toward the living room.

The man turned. Buster stood his ground a few feet away from Trugman, barking and growling.

"Don't shoot the dog!" Dad said. "Let me go to him."

Keeping an eye on Dad and Bullet Face, Trugman slowly stepped back.

"Don't move or I'll put one in ya," he said to Dad.

Micheline was behind me, holding my wrapped left hand.

"He won't attack unless you attack us," Dad said. "Just relax and he'll relax."

"Fuck that."

Without a thought, I broke free of Micheline and ran out. I was holding the Walther like Dad taught me, hands firmly on the grip and extended out.

"Don't shoot my dog," was all I could think to say.

"What the hell is this?"

"Graham, go back to your room," Dad ordered. "Now!" He looked at Trugman. "That's just a BB gun. Just a little BB gun."

He aimed the revolver directly at Dad.

"Kid, I'm going to put a bullet right through your dad's head if you don't stop right there and drop that pea shooter."

"It's a Walther LP53," I told him bravely.

"Graham, go to your room, now. Everything is okay here."

The captain kept the gun pointed at Dad.

"Listen to your dad, son," Bullet Face said.

"This is ridiculous," Trugman said. "Kid, the most you're going to do with that is sting me. I can see the air cartridge where the magazine should be. Now drop it and hold your dog back or I'll shoot your dad. Now."

I kept the Walther pointed at him and grabbed Buster by the collar. His hair was standing up and he was trying to pull away from me.

"This was supposed to be simple. Where's the maid?"

"I am here," she said as she stepped out from the hall and walked to my side.

"Damn—and I believed you, Sanderson."

"We still have a good arrangement," Bullet Face said. "You can walk out of here. No one needs to get hurt."

I don't think Trugman heard the man. He seemed more worried about Buster than me. He didn't order me again to drop the pellet pistol, so I didn't.

"I don't want to have to shoot anyone else today, especially your kid. I'm going to walk out of here. Easy peasy."

He moved the revolver to his left hand and unholstered the other pistol with his right. Pointed it at Dad. He tossed the .38 behind him a few feet, almost in the den.

Buster jerked free the moment the gun hit the floor. Ran toward Trugman, who turned to shoot. I pointed the pistol at his head and without having a sight on anything, I pulled the trigger.

The pellet hit him right in the left eye.

"My eye!" he screamed. "My damn eye. Aww shit!"

Dad and Bullet Face were on him a split second later, taking him to the ground. Dad kept punching him in the face while Bullet Face held his legs down. Buster was biting and tearing into his right arm.

The man was screaming, and a few seconds later stopped. Dad kept punching him. Bullet Face stood up and retrieved the pistol from the floor. He slapped Dad on the back.

"Get up, Sanderson. He's done."

Dad punched him hard in his bloodied face one more time and then stood. Buster was still tearing away at his bloody arm, growling like he did when he was ripping up a tug-of-war rag after jerking it away from me.

Dad grabbed him by the collar and pulled him off.

I looked at Mr. Stankey. He had a bullet hole in his forehead. Blood and little beads of brain and flesh were pasted to the wall behind him.

"I'll have to be more careful about who I let drive me," said Bullet Face.

FIFTY-EIGHT

You always remember the first man you shot. The Walther was powerful. The pellet took his eye out. I didn't gloat. Far from it. I had a hard time falling asleep. Knowing Buster was there helped. Strange to me how he could turn so violent but curl up with me at night. He was my boy. My best friend.

I couldn't figure out at the time what I was feeling, but it has stayed with me to this day.

A few days later, Dad told me that Roddy and his mom had been taken to a safe house provided by the CIA until they could return to the States. I never saw Roddy again. I tried to call him before he left, but his mom said he didn't want to talk to me. Was I responsible for his dad's death? I was. In my young mind I was responsible. It didn't matter that my dad believed me and followed through with it at the end. His believing me was all that mattered, before Mr. Stankey died.

There was a man who worked for the CIA. He was assigned to stay in our apartment when Dad was gone. He mostly sat in the living room on a chair that faced the front door. Hardly like he was there at all. He read magazines and occasionally spent time talking on the phone. Didn't sound official. More like talking to someone like his wife. Other than that, he was all business. Brought his own lunches and snacks, except for coffee; Micheline always made him a pot. He never had to use the bathroom, either. I found that odd. I wondered if the CIA trained them to hold it.

The curfew was still in place. Lenny called. Said that he'd heard what happened, but the details weren't clear. Micheline said he could visit. He came down right away and we went to my room.

"You have a bodyguard?"

"Yeah, I guess."

"Poor ol' Roddy. You ever talk to him?"

"No. You?"

"No, he wouldn't talk to me."

"Me either. They're not here anymore, anyway," I said.

"Man, that sucks. I can't believe what happened!"

"Me either."

"So tell me everything."

"I'd rather not right now."

"You gotta give me something. Did your dad shoot the bad guy?"

"Naw."

"Did you see Mr. Stankey when he was dead?"

"No," I lied. "I was in my room with Micheline when it all happened."

"Damn, must've been something else."

"I can't stop thinking about Roddy, Lenny."

"I know. Me too. You think he'll ever come back?"

"Dad said they're going back to the States to stay with family. Don't see a reason why they'd come back."

"So you musta seen the body when you left your room."

"Lenny, stop it with that shit. I didn't see anything."

"All right, all right. Calm down. Man."

"Roddy lost his dad, for cripes' sake."

"I know—and it's not like I don't feel really bad for him."

"Well, it sure as hell sounds like it. All you're interested in is dead bodies."

"That's not *all* I'm interested in."

"Then quit asking about it."

"All right, already."

At first I thought I'd be able to tell him everything, but for some reason I couldn't. I didn't know why. That was the only reason he wanted to come down to my apartment, though. He stayed for a short while. I couldn't find anything to talk to him about, and what he had to talk about was of no interest to me anymore. I didn't hang out with him much after that. We went our separate ways. I never made any other friends in Beirut. The curfew didn't help, and most of the other kids in our building were older teenagers or adults.

Dad always returned in time for dinner. He rarely worked late anymore. He never bothered to hide his satchel either. He left it on the floor in the foyer. I knew what was in it but didn't have the desire to hold it anymore.

We were eating on dinner trays in the living room again.

"Can you take me to see the Pigeon Man?"

He shot me a knowing look, like he could read me.

"Of course." He smiled.

"Can we go up there on Saturday? He's usually exercising the pigeons in the morning."

"Yes," was all he said, then continued eating.

"Should I bring him something?"

"I think your presence will be enough. He doesn't strike me as a man that needs or wants anything."

"I want him to sign my cast."

"We'll see if he will. Don't get your hopes up."

"I won't."

We ate the rest of our dinner in silence.

The next day we walked halfway up the Stinky Steps. A narrow path on the right led to the Pigeon Man's shack. The pigeons were not out, but I could see him sitting on a chair beside the shack.

"I'll wait here," Dad said.

"But I want you to come with me."

"You should do this on your own. I'll be right here."

The Pigeon Man noticed me as I walked the path toward him. He stood.

There were several pigeon coops made of wood and mesh outside the front door to his shack and near the wooden chair he was sitting on. The pigeons were cooing comfortably and perched on wooden dowels that looked handmade.

I waved. He didn't wave back. He placed his right hand on his chest over his heart and bowed his head slightly.

"*Marhaba*," I said.

He said something I didn't understand. It was longer than a simple hello.

"I just wanted to say thank you. *Shukran*."

He smiled and nodded, directed me toward the pigeon coops with his hand, then raised both of his hands above his head. He said something else, walked toward the coops, and opened each door. When the last door was opened, he stepped back and the pigeons flew out in sync, inches from me. I was fanned by their wings as they flew up and began circling over the shack.

"Wow," was all I could think to say.

He smiled. I pulled a pen from my right pants pocket, showed him my cast with all the writing and signatures on it. I mimed writing something on the cast with the pen, stretched my hand out after to offer it to him.

"Sign my cast?" I asked.

It seemed like he didn't understand, or maybe couldn't figure out why I would want him to sign the cast, but when I handed him the pen, he took the cap off. I stretched out my arm. He held it gently underneath with his left hand and wrote something in Arabic. It appeared to be something more than a name. When he finished, he put the cap back on the pen and handed it to me with a smile.

"*Shukran,*" I said again, then stretched out my hand to shake. He took it with both hands and held it. He smiled again. I turned and walked back toward my dad. When I got to the steps, I waved at him. He waved back. I showed Dad the cast.

"Is this his name?" I asked.

"We'll have to get it translated."

I picked up a strong stick on the way down, used it like a walking stick.

"Can we stop by the fort?" I asked.

"Why do you want to go there?"

"I need to do something."

When we got to the fort I didn't look inside. I shoved the stick through the top with my good hand and pulled it toward me, breaking some of the branches apart.

"Why did you do that?"

"Have to."

After that I beat around the opening as hard as I could until the branches closed in on it. I shoved the big stick through the top again—a sword into the heart of the fort—and left it there.

We walked back to the building. The concierge was sitting on a chair to the left of the elevator when we returned. He spoke enough English to get by. Dad asked him if he could translate the writing on my cast.

I showed it to him.

"Peace be upon you," he said.

FIFTY-NINE

The fighting in Lebanon intensified. Gunfire and explosions throughout the day and into the night.

One of those nights, after dinner, Dad said, "The embassy is evacuating people."

"What do you mean?"

"You're going to have to go back to the States and live with your mom until I return."

"You're not coming with me?"

"I have to stay for a while, but I'll go with you and Buster to the airport to see you off. Your mother will pick you up at the airport in New York."

"I don't want to go."

"You have to, Graham. It's not safe here anymore."

"Then why are you staying?"

"Because it's my job. Only for a few weeks. I'll have everything packed up and sent back to the States. You just pack what you need."

"You mean now?"

"You're leaving in the morning. Pack some clothes tonight."

"I don't want to live with Mom."

"Don't give me a hard time with this, okay? You have to go and I don't want any argument from you. Understood?"

"Yeah, I guess."

"You guess?"

"Yes, I understand. What about Micheline?"

"She'll stay here until everything is packed. I'll make sure she gets settled somewhere."

"She can't go with me?"

"No. The government won't pay for her."

"Then you pay for her."

"I can't, Graham. She has to stay."

"She's like family."

"And I'll make sure she's safe."

I called Lenny later.

"I'm being evacuated," I told him.

"Me too."

"When do you have to leave?"

"Tomorrow. I was going to give you a call, but you beat me to it."

"It feels weird."

"Yeah, I know. I gotta get back to packing. My dad said you can get in touch with me using the State Department's address, care of my dad's name."

"My dad has his name."

"I guess I'll talk to you later, then."

"I guess."

It was still dark that next morning. Alem helped me with my luggage. He lifted the bags into the trunk of the sedan. Micheline was there. She was crying.

"I will go with him," she said to Dad.

"I can't make that happen, Micheline," Dad said calmly.

I couldn't look at her. I felt ashamed. She came to me, though, wrapped her arms around me, and held me. She still smelled like coconut oil. It was a comforting smell.

"We have to go, Micheline," Dad said.

She wouldn't let go.

"I will go with him. Take care of your home."

"We have to go. Get in the car, son."

I felt the tears come. I tried to stop from crying, but couldn't. She let me go and I quickly got into the backseat with Buster and held him.

"Don't leave me here, Mr. Sanderson. Please don't leave me here."

"Go to the apartment, Micheline. I'll be back soon."

He got in the front seat and we drove away. I looked in the rearview mirror and could see her on her knees, sobbing. The image of her never left me.

SIXTY

Dad had everything shipped to a storage facility in Virginia. He drove up from there to New York, where we were living with some cousins, but stayed in a hotel. They were soon divorced. I thought I would live with my dad, but my mother was given custody of both me and Tommy, and then Dad got the assignment I knew he wanted: Saigon. He wrote us a lot of letters, called when he could, and always made sure to send us cards with twenty bucks in them for our birthdays and Christmas.

I was sixteen in 1975 when my dad returned from Saigon after it fell. Mom and Tommy and I were living in an apartment in Arlington, Virginia. My dad returned to the condo in DC. I went to live with him there because, according to my mother, I was too much to handle and always getting into trouble. That was not untrue. I had fallen in with the wrong crowd in Arlington, and she could not control me—certainly couldn't tell me what to do or when I had to be home. Living with my dad set me straight. I did well my last two years of high school and got accepted into George Washington University.

I had not really thought about Beirut since becoming an adult. It wasn't until the last few years that I started to reminisce. Being a kid there, amid all the violence, was nothing more than an adventure. Didn't realize that lives were being lost, families displaced, and a city was in the throes of near-destruction. Just a grand adventure. Witnessing the murder was different, though. Seeing death close-up. Roddy's dad was worse. It changed me. Watching my dad beat the shit out of that man. I know he would have killed him if Bullet Face had not pulled him off. I've felt that kind of rage. Thankfully, I have never killed anyone in that state of mind.

I thought about trying to find Roddy but feared opening old wounds. I found Lenny, through Facebook. He was a PE teacher at a high school in Akron, Ohio, still married and with three older kids. We always talked about getting together, but we never did. Time got away from us and he became just another Facebook friend.

Frightening how fast it flew by. When you're a kid, the days are long, but time has a way of speeding up the older you get. That's why it feels like Beirut was not all that long ago, far from a distant memory.

I still have my cast. It has turned a yellow with age. I keep it on a shelf in my home office, the Star of David necklace folded over it. *Peace be upon you* is something I'm still hoping for.

ABOUT THE AUTHOR

David Swinson grew up in Washington, DC; Beirut; Mexico City; Mallorca; and Stockholm; the son of a foreign service officer. He is a retired police detective from the Metropolitan Police Department in Washington, DC, having been assigned to Major Crimes. Swinson is the author of *The Second Girl*, *Crime Song*, and *Trigger*. He lives in Northern Virginia with his wife, daughter, Staffordshire terrier, and Moose, the micro pig.